THE LAWBRINGERS

THE LAWBRINGERS

by Brian Wynne Garfield

NEW YORK—THE MACMILLAN COMPANY

A DIVISION OF THE CROWELL-COLLIER PUBLISHING COMPANY

1962

First Printing

Printed in the United States of America

Library of Congress catalog card number: 62-18377

The Macmillan Company, New York

Collier Macmillan Canada Limited, Galt, Ontario

This book is respectfully dedicated to
the memory of Burton C. Mossman—a
chivalrous gentleman, a lawman and an
Arizonan.

—Brian Wynne Garfield
Tucson, 1961

CONTENTS

CONTENTS

AUTHOR'S NOTE

This novel is suggested by the life of Burton C. Mossman (1867–1956) and the brief but important span of years during which he lived in Arizona.

At the turn of the present century Arizona was far behind the nation in terms of codified justice, peace, safety, protection of rights, social cultivation and political maturity. The population was scattered thinly across the Territory and laws were often no more than what a man—an individual man—could make of them. Frequently enough, justice was measured in physical hardiness and marksmanship; and still Arizonans felt their Territory should be accepted by the United States Government as a

AUTHOR'S NOTE

State of the Union. To win this acceptance, they had to tame their land, and they had to tame it quickly.

Forces that were sometimes directly opposed to one another worked to bring reasonable order to the chaos that was Arizona in 1901. Transition was to come rapidly from the old rugged ruthlessness to the newer realization of a growing need for conscience, social responsibility and more mature cultivation.

This novel deals with those who represented the forces at work in transition—those who tamed the land. Most of the men and women in this novel were real; unfortunately I have not personally met many of them, but have learned of them not only from bibliographic sources but also from anecdotes related to me by those who did know them.

It might be mentioned here that, while in recent years the bloody and violent aspects of life in the American West have been overemphasized to a ridiculous extreme, still the wild and woolly adventures of the West certainly took place, and not just occasionally. Almost all vintage commentaries and diaries, not to mention pioneer newspapers and contemporary historians, have illustrated this fact beyond doubt.

The West's frontier violence extended from the seventeenth century, when pioneers fought skirmishes with Indians, well into the early years of the twentieth century. Gunplay and roughshod "Colt's Law" did not end abruptly at the magic date 1900. For example, as late as 1913, on Broad Street in Globe, Arizona, three gunfights took place within the space of one week, each resulting in someone's death. This is hardly an isolated example of Southwestern life in the raw. The period of time contained within this novel (1901–1903) was marked particularly by blatant outlawry and rough justice of hemp and gunpowder in Arizona Territory.

My indebtedness must be expressed to my fellow members of the Western Writers of America, Inc., who have kindly encouraged my work; to Douglas D. Martin, for his friendship and his ideas; to Dr. John A. Carroll, eminent Southwestern historian, for inspiration; to the Arizona Pioneers' Historical Society and to the University of Arizona, my alma mater and the home of many documents used in the preparation of this novel; to Robert Ramsey, Jack Huggins and Dr. Patrick McCarthy, for advice and encouragement; to countless authors and editors who have published material contributing to the Mossman story; particularly to Frazier Hunt, whom I have never met, who is the author of *CAP MOSSMAN: Last of the Great Cowmen* (a biography), published in New York by Hastings House in 1951; and to Gwynne Cox Allen and Frances O'Brien, who suffered through the reading of the manuscript.

—Brian Wynne Garfield
Tucson, 1961

CHAPTER I

SANTEE SMITH

It was, he thought idly, the sixteenth of April. There was a quiet, threatening loneliness about the desert country. With the muscles of his back tensed against a bullet that might come any time, Santee Smith reined in his horse and had a look over his shoulder.

The unfriendly white glare of the powdered ground beat against his slitted eyes. With some relief he saw that not a moving dot showed anywhere on the whole expanse of the plain behind him. His attention swept all the way back to the blurred violet of distant peaks, but in all that area not a single spire gave away the presence of riders. On this rounded, treeless hilltop, the wind moved gently

1

by, cooling his sweat-damp skin and roughing up his hair when he lifted his hat. The brassy sun glared harshly in his face; the sky was steel-blue and nowhere could he see a cloud except far to the south, over the mountain summits, where he found the gray, lined streaks of heavily falling rain.

He felt the push of time driving him forward. Somewhere behind him a group of men rode, seeking his trail. If he had been asked he would have said nothing about it, but actually Santee was afraid. Below him were the heavy cottonwood banks at the edge of the muddy Santa Cruz River, running narrow and thin. After one more careful survey of the empty land westward, he put the horse downslope to the river and let it quench its thirst while he slipped out of the saddle and knelt to cup water in his hands. He drank and washed. Quite specific, the fragrance of wild honeysuckle reached his nostrils; and since that was an unusual thing, he squatted motionless, enjoying it. Mixed with it he smelled the leather-sweat of long saddle travel on his faded Levis. He tarried briefly there, then mounted and splashed across the river's shallow flow, threaded the cottonwoods beyond and pressed eastward through the hills.

It was a shrinking in his belly, the creeping knowledge that no matter how far he traveled, sometime and somewhere Creed Jacks and Chacon would find him. He shrugged as though he were a tough man and glanced at the sky. The wind was from the south, which was where the clouds lay, dark and distant. *To hell with Creed Jacks,* he thought; *to hell with Chacon. Nobody's that tough— only takes one bullet. Those two can get pleats in their skulls just as easy as the next man.*

Stringing the words together was easy enough, but it did not send away the tightness in his belly. He looked over his shoulder again. All he could see was the mica-white country jogging past. The trail carried him upward across alkali flats, up past a sentinel rock outcrop and higher into mountain country; the flats gave way to brush, the brush to scrub trees, the scrubs to timber, and presently, after another two hours' travel, he topped the summit of a pass and halted to look down his back trail again. Nothing stirred in sight. A hawk cruised by, not beating its wings. The wind, cool and hollow, cut across this unprotected summit with a sharp edge that sliced through Santee's shirt. The land fell away from him in all directions, tilting and swooping like the hawk. The tops of lodgepole pines like lances at drill poked up from the slopes descending from his post. Santee sat there awhile with the wind brushing his cheeks and something about the feel of this high mountaintop made the fear drop more heavily into the pit of his stomach. He remembered Creed Jacks and he knew Creed was on his trail now, although he had not seen any sign of Creed or anyone else during the past twenty-four hours of riding. He looked down the mountain, the way he had just come, but there was still no one in sight and no one on the flats far below, and so he put his horse down the trail and left the high pass.

During the course of two days' travel he could not shake his fear. By the time he reached Bisbee shortly before noon the next day, he was so weary of his own anxieties that he said aloud: "To hell with it. Let them come." And looked for a stable.

On the edge of the mountains, the town was weathered and dried. Turbulent heat and loose dust lay along the surface of the irregular street he traveled, even though he knew it had snowed in these hills a week ago. A scatter of horses stood around, hipshot and half asleep on their feet, and a stagecoach, probably from Tombstone, rocked around the corner and pitched to a stop at a hotel not far from the railroad depot. It was a big town but it was sleeping and almost dead, except for the mines where men worked like ants.

Santee rode around the stagecoach and went on as far as the wide-mouthed adobe livery barn. He rode inside before he stepped down in the shade. The hostler was an old and wrinkled Indian with a square face the color of old copper. He pushed forward from the rear gloom where he had been forking hay, and Santee said: "Rub him down and walk him around some."

"Si."

Manure stench was strong in the hot, close air. "Then give him a bag of oats and stall him."

"Si."

"You're a talky gent," Santee observed.

"Si."

Santee grinned. "How much? *Cuanto?*"

"*Cincuentos-centavos-de-Los-Estados.*" The old Indian ran it all together but Santee pieced it out and tossed him a half-dollar.

"Much obliged," he told the hostler, and walked back toward the street, a tall and weary young man. At twenty-three he had the lean hips of a horseman and the wide, flat-sinewed back of a man who worked with his muscles. His skin was dust-dry and carved like old leather, so that he seemed fifteen years older than he was; his hair was a sun-bleached sandy color where it stuck out in unruly licks from under his hat brim. Santee's face was ordinary enough except for his nose, which was a long flat blade, and his eyes, which were transparently blue like the sky and half-shuttered most of the time with squint-wrinkles at the edges, from looking across the open desert under the Arizona sun.

He couldn't help pausing in the stable doorway's shadow to survey both ends of the street. But, he thought, if Chacon and Creed Jacks came this way at all, it would be a long time before they figured out the crazy trail he'd left them back along Turkey Creek.

A little ashamed of his timidity, he stepped boldly out into the sun. His spurs dragged the walk and he paused to unbuckle them and slip them over the handle of his holstered revolver. He shifted the weight of his saddlebags from one shoulder to the other and looked around the town. A ranch buckboard rocked past and as soon as the dust had settled Santee crossed the street to stand in the shade cast by a new brick bank building while he decided what to do next.

He reflected with some bitterness that he was beginning to stink almost as much, and as offensively, as a wet saddle blanket. He needed a bath, a shave, a haircut, and a chance to change into the clean clothes in his saddlebags. After that he would get a meal and sleep around the clock, and finally he would look for a job. He needed a job; his money was low.

One sign a hundred feet away said TONSORIAL PARLOR and he went that way. He dropped the saddlebags in the corner, climbed into the chair and shut his eyes when the barber tied an apron and towel around him. While the scissors clipped his hair crisply, the barber's voice drifted across his weary thoughts, "Need any tooth work?"

"Not so's you'd notice it."

The barber grunted. "Stranger?"

"Believe I am."

The barber grunted again. The scissors clipped, and stopped; the barber covered his chin with warm, moist lather and stropped his razor with loud slaps. "Just passing through?"

Santee thought about it. He thought of Creed Jacks and Chacon; he thought, *I can't run far enough to leave them behind.* And so he said, "Not if I can get a job."

"What kind of job?"

"I ain't in a position to choose."

"The marshal's looking for a new deputy. He lost one of his men last week. It don't pay much."

Santee considered it. "Who's the marshal?"

"Graham."

"Dayton Graham?"

"That's the one."

"What's he need a deputy for?"

"This is a big town. He's got half a dozen."

"How'd he lose the last one?"

"Shot," the barber said complacently. "That's why the job's still open."

"I see," Santee muttered; he didn't move his jaw when he spoke because the razor was scraping his skin drily. *Shot,* he thought. Still, the possibility might offer advantages. Under Dayton Graham's expert wing, a man might be reasonably safe from riders like Creed Jacks and the Chacon crew. It was worth consideration. He said, "Obliged for the information."

"*De nada,*" the barber said.

His cheeks smooth, his hair neat, Santee went into the place's back room, poured a few buckets of stove-hot water into the cast-iron tub that sat squatly in the room's center, took off his clothes and settled gently into the steaming bath. With the tub soaped up into a lather, he sat back and thought about the prospect of walking the streets of Bisbee town with a gun and a badge. Bisbee was a tough town.

He was like that, scrubbed raw and soaking in the steam-warmth, when a fusillade of shots made him snap up his head and listen.

They were too many, the gunshots, and too close together to be mistaken for a bunch of cowboys on a spree. The heavy drum of hoofbeats rose and swept away, diminishing into silence. Outside, through the thin walls, he heard men's voices rising in excitement, and the confused milling of movement. Presently someone spoke a quick command and another body of horsemen galloped away. The furor diminished. By this time Santee was in his fresh clothes and pulling his boots on. He went through the door into the front of the barbershop. No one was there. But as he advanced he saw the front door swing open, and the barber came in, shaking his head. Santee said: "What's all the ruction?"

"Holdup," the barber said. "Chacon and his crowd. Held up the hardware store—shot old man Hackett."

"Dead?"

"No. But he may be soon. He's got a hole through his throat. Graham took a posse out on their trail."

"How many?"

"The posse?"

"No, damn it. Chacon's crew."

"Oh," the barber said. "There was six of them."

Santee nodded. That represented Chacon's full comple-ment, including Creed Jacks. Santee went to the doorway and stood in it, resting his shoulder against the jamb. Chacon's crew obviously had come here looking for him, for Santee, but they'd seen something else that they must have decided they wanted more, so they took it; and for the moment they forgot Santee. It had to be that way.

"Guess you'll have to wait for the marshal to get back if you want to talk about that job. Nobody ever caught up to Dayton Graham once he got out on the trail." The bar-ber grinned without mirth.

"I guess so." Santee handed him two dollars and turned out onto the boardwalk, which ran only the length of this block of Main Street and turned up Brewery Gulch. He stood a moment; he thought: *I may as well. This town's as safe as anywhere.* "And," he added aloud, "a job's a job."

"What?"

"Nothing," he said to the barber, and walked up the street. He paused at the Plaza, which was Bisbee's center of activity, and had a look around. He had been here be-fore but that had been some time ago and the town had grown. The Copper Queen and the C & A mines were op-erating at full capacity, bringing up gold and silver and copper all at once. Men walked past him on the street, most of them thick-bodied miners from Prussia and Ire-land and Italy and Spain, dressed in coveralls and squint-ing curiously as men did who spent most of their day un-derground.

Up the street from here was the railroad depot and the foot of Brewery Gulch, and the beginning of the road leading down out of Mule Pass to the Mexican Border a few miles away. Santee stood near the steps of the post office and turned, looking up Main Street toward Tombstone Canyon, and saw more pedestrians crisscrossing the dirt road, most of them likewise miners. Bisbee boasted a population somewhere between six and ten thousand; it was hard to tell from day to day. But one thing seemed fairly certain to Santee: none of the men in sight seemed dangerous to him. So he ignored them; he went into the English Kitchen and ate a steak and black-fried potatoes; he went on to the Turf Saloon and had two drinks; he came back to the Plaza, idling, wishing the posse would return, and finally turned into the lobby of a small hotel, where he set down his saddlebags and sat on a wooden chair, his legs extended before him, and opened a week-old newspaper. Weariness pulled his shoulders down and slumped him in his seat. His lips moved while he read slowly. Once he shifted his seat. In half an hour he put the newspaper away and picked up a copy of the Tucson *Star*. Now and then his eyebrows lifted with interest. The clock hands above the desk revolved and chimes struck at intervals. Men drifted in and out, one or two at a time, and he was on the point of going out for a restless walk when his eyes touched a copy of an illustrated weekly across the room, and he went to it.

He was half through a lurid tale of Buffalo Bill when a small commotion occurred outside—a number of horses arriving—and someone on the porch said, "Any luck, Marshal?"

"They're across the Border. We trailed them to Naco." The voice was tired and noncommittal; the horses drummed away down the street. Santee frowned, wishing

Chacon's bunch hadn't got away. Presently he folded the magazine, stood up and stretched, and walked outside. Dust still hung in the air, turning everything in sight to yellow. A trio of horsemen just then breasted the far end of the street and swept forward past the squat 'dobes and wooden buildings, coming to a halt before the post office building a block away. The three riders stepped down and went inside. One of them was short and trim and looked, at this distance, vaguely familiar. The marshal's posse had tied its horses up there too, and assuming the marshal was in one of the offices there, Santee stepped away from the hotel and went forward. His boots kicked up little eddies of dust. The sun was on its way down; it was just four hours since the hardware store robbery. He mounted the far sidewalk and cruised along to the post office, stopping by the six steps to look inside a high window. His eyes just cleared the bottom of the sill; this long old building was built high to withstand Apache attacks and floods coming down the gulches. Santee's eyes widened and his lips formed a soundless word: "Mossman. Think of that, now."

That was Burt Mossman inside, with the marshal and two other men. Santee stopped fast where he was. *Something new to think about—damn!* Through the dusty window he watched Mossman and tried to gauge the man's mood.

Mossman was talking to the marshal. His lips moved but no sound came through the pane. Mossman's gray eyes, as always, were speculative—asking silent questions; otherwise his face was gravely wooden. He had to look up at the marshal, for he was no more than five feet nine in his boots; his build was solidly muscled and there was a defensive jut to his jaw that made his whole face seem cut from granite. A full-swept cavalry-style mustache guarded his lips, dark and twisted. Santee could not judge Mossman's temper; he could only watch, and wonder. Mossman's eyes were coolly, brightly gray, bold but not malicious in the way they held the marshal's. There was an intensity about Mossman, a fineness and a powerful suggestion of latent anger under layers of quiet courtesy. Santee thought, *It was a long time ago, but he'll remember.* What should a man do?

He was still like that, uncertain and alert, when Mossman turned with an abrupt snap of his shoulders and walked out of view, trailed closely by Marshal Graham. Thereupon the door at the head of the stairs opened, and before Santee had time to decide his next action, Mossman appeared on the steps. Mossman saw him immediately. His face moved; his eyes were as impersonal as a snake's.

"Hello, Santee."

Santee dipped his head with cautious politeness. Mossman seemed almost willing to let it go at that; he came down the stairs and turned halfway and seemed about to speak to the marshal at his shoulder; but then his attention came around again. "Santee."

"What?"

"Know anything about Chacon?"

"Maybe," Santee said; he was unsure and unwilling to commit himself. Mossman's gray eyes glittered steadily; ripples formed and went away at his jaw. He stepped forward. "I won't accept that, boy."

Santee moved back a pace; Mossman stayed with him. He felt uncomfortable under Mossman's unwinking gaze. "All right," he said quickly; "all right."

"You've seen him," Mossman said. "Recently."

"Yes."

Mossman stood motionless. Then his hand lifted; he removed his hat and pressed the back of his wrist to his forehead, mopping the oil of sweat away. Then he put his hat on. The silence lasted that long, a studied stillness, after which Mossman boosted him gently, "Tell me about it, boy."

"I was running some O-Bar cows out of the Breaks," Santee said.

"What for?"

Santee flushed. "For O-Bar. I was working for the O-Bar."

The half-lidded intensity of Mossman's eyes troubled him. He went on: "Chacon and his bunch tried to take the O-Bar cows away from us. The O-Bar ramrod had given us orders to shoot at rustlers, so Hector Soto and I gave them a fight."

"And?"

"We shot at them," Santee said. "Soto was dead before the first volley ended. I had to take cover in the rocks, and then I started sniping at them. I hit one man."

"Who?"

"Creed Jacks's brother—Judah."

"Ah," Mossman said. "I see. Go on."

"Then the rest of Chacon's crew ran away."

"With the O-Bar herd?"

"Just so," Santee admitted.

"Was Creed Jacks with Chacon?"

"Sure."

"I thought Creed was a friend of yours."

"That was a long time ago."

"All right," Mossman murmured. "What then?"

"I walked down to look over the field. Soto was dead and so was Creed's brother. I hoofed back to headquarters and picked up my horse."

"So you rode away," Mossman said.

"What you expect me to do? I killed Creed's brother, damn it! I'd have been forty different kinds of fool if I'd stayed there and just waited for them to hunt me down."

Mossman's eyes did not blink. Marshal Graham flanked him, a tall curly wolf, his skin wind-carved; Graham stood with an indolent pose, not saying anything, not even watching Santee. The muscles of Santee's stomach tightened. "Look. I hired on with the O-Bar to work cows and do chores. Not to fight off Chacon's bunch all by myself. Besides, the O-Bar's down to less than a thousand cows now, what with drought and rustlers. They don't need a five-man crew—they can't support it. Somebody had to quit."

"You never did stick to anything long," Mossman said.

"That ain't fair," Santee said, coloring.

Mossman moved his head in polite disagreement. His voice had a depth and a confident resonance: "It's been some time since you rode with that crew of Jack-Mormon rustlers on Hashknife. Changed any, Santee?"

"I hope so."

Mossman's eyes swept him as they might have swept an open hand of cards or a horse for sale. It was a thorough and unhurried inspection. Santee began to feel jumpy. Mossman said, "You used to have nerve."

"There's a difference between nerve and damn foolishness. I won't stand and fight six rifles. That don't take nerve—it takes a crazy man."

"A fact," Mossman murmured, still watching him intently in that curious, discomforting way. Mossman's eyebrows lowered slightly, making a straight dark line across his eyes. He had small hands and small feet and he probably didn't weigh more than 165 pounds, yet strength was as plain on him as the sun-dark color of his skin. Soberly disturbed and uncertain, Santee was unable to look away. He dragged the back of his hand across his lips and he heard his own voice, awkward and strained, "What do you want from me?"

"Don't spook." Mossman's eyes held him for such a length of time that Santee became afraid to look away, even to blink; there was this contest of wills between them. Santee felt the beginning salt of tears in his eyes. That was when Mossman said, quickly and surely: "I need another man to ride with me. Do you want a job?"

Santee jerked his glance away. "What job? What kind of job?"

"Law work."

Santee's expression shifted to Marshal Graham, a tall and silent fighter, and back to Mossman. "Something new and different," Santee murmured. "Tell me about it."

"You've heard of the Rangers?"

"Just in Texas," Santee said.

Mossman smiled slightly. "We've just started."

"Who's 'we'?"

"I," Mossman said, "am the Arizona Rangers."

Santee just looked at him. Then he said: "Judas. I never heard."

"Now you've heard."

"You're offering a Ranger job to me?"

"Yes."

Santee blinked. "Think of that."

"If you take it," Mossman said evenly, "your first assignment will be to ride with us after Chacon."

"How many others in the bunch?"

"You, me, and two others."

"That's a tall order."

Mossman turned his body half around. "We're leaving now. If you don't want it, make your position plain."

"They're in Mexico," Santee said. "You can't follow them into Mexico."

Mossman's only answer was a vague upturn of his lip corners.

"It ain't legal," Santee insisted.

"Then take it up with the courts," Mossman said. "Judge Williams's office is just up the stairs here. I've got no time to argue legalities, Santee. Get your horse or drop out."

Mossman was already moving, on his way to the horses tied at the wooden rack.

"Why," Santee said uncertainly, "it might be fun at that."

"Come on, then."

"All right," he said. "All right."

CHAPTER II

POLITICS ON THE FRONTIER

Judge Starr Williams paused for breath halfway up the steps of the capitol building in Phoenix. For a spring day it seemed cool; the only clouds in sight lay close over the southern horizon, white with gray centers. Tilted on its leather springs, a mud wagon mail coach rocked past in the street at the foot of the steps. A harsh report issued from the lower end of the city, sending staccato echoes crashing around in the air; and after listening a moment, Judge Williams said aloud, "Some fool cowboy shooting off his gun," and faced upward once more. He counted steps as he climbed, "Six, seven, eight," and walked between Grecian pillars into the central corridor.

It wasn't even as old as his own house; it was two years old—the capital had only moved to Phoenix from Prescott in '99; yet he stood in the wide hall showing his teeth, disliking the building's hostile coldness. He removed his wide, flat-crowned gray beaver hat and held it under his thumb. His heels sent crisp echoes back along the floor; he walked straight through to the corridor's end, made a series of turns and stood before the clerk's desk in the executive outer office.

The clerk was middle-aged and sallow. He owned watery eyes and a ragged, unsuccessful brown mustache. The judge said, "I've had a message from Governor Murphy," and, out of habit, handed the clerk his card.

"Sit down; it will be just a minute." The clerk rose and turned out of the room through a thick oak door.

Judge Williams sat in a maroon leather chair, put his document case down beside him, crossed his legs and carefully hung his hat over one knee. He lifted a thin, strong hand to bring out his watch, and thought, *It's a long trip from Bisbee here.* He glanced idly around the room, at the silly decorations and the littered disorder of the clerk's desk, at the emptiness of half a dozen heavy maroon chairs; he thought, *Come on—come on, now.*

The clerk reappeared with a hushed and reverent air and went to his desk before he spoke, never looking at the judge. "The governor will see you," he said in a tone of stiff courtesy, and picked up a pencil.

He carries Philadelphia around him like a shell, Judge Williams thought. *Only this isn't Philadelphia.* He said two dry words, "Thank you," and went past the desk with his case and hat. He closed the oak door behind him and saw immediately that besides the governor, two other men were present: Colonel Epes Randolph, the railroader, and E. S. Ives, president of the Territorial Senate. *Impressive company*, the judge thought; he stood on the carpet and said, "Good afternoon."

Governor Murphy looked up from his desk and waved a hand. "Hello, Starr. Sit down—I'll only be a minute. You know these gentlemen?"

"Yes," the judge said. He shook hands with Randolph, who was thick-chested and aggressive of chin, and with Ives, who had a look of polished competence; and he took a seat in a high-backed wooden chair by the wall. Through the window behind the governor's bent head he could see the round hump of Camelback Mountain, and farther on the misty blue of the jagged Superstitions. Somewhere down in town dust milled up in a spire. The judge cleared his throat and put his hat on the seat of the chair beside him, and smiled at the uncomfortable expressions of Ives and Randolph.

Governor Murphy put away his pen and thrust his chair back, relaxing his stocky frame. He touched his sideburns and folded his hands over his ample torso. "I'm sorry to keep you waiting, gentlemen."

"It's a busy day," said Ives, a little petulantly.

"I'm sorry, then," the governor said again. "You two gentlemen know the cause of this meeting. I don't think Judge Williams knows."

"I don't," the judge said, and kept his interested attention on the governor's florid face.

"I'll explain for the judge's benefit," Governor Murphy said; he stood up, thrusting his massive stomach forward, and rested one hand against the corner of his desk. "You'll remember, I'm sure, the catastrophe of some eighteen years ago when the extent of organized banditry in Cochise County became so overwhelming that the Federal Government was forced to declare a state of martial law there."

"I remember it," the judge said. "Go on, Governor."

"At that time, this Territory earned an impressively disgusting reputation. We were the laughingstock of the country, and every Eastern newspaper ridiculed us."

"What you're getting at," the judge said, "is that we're approaching the same situation again."

"I'm afraid we are." The governor moved back to stand by the window, and looked out over Phoenix town while he spoke. His hands lay clasped behind his back. The governor's brows, the judge noted lately, were knitted much more often. Governor Murphy blinked and spoke slowly:

"In Eastern opinion, Arizona is again becoming an overgrown den of thieves. We're what Texas was after the War Between the States, and what the Indian Territory was ten years ago. We've become the most popular outlaw hideout in the world. I wouldn't be surprised if the number of honest citizens we have isn't almost matched by the number of toughs dodging the law. It's not safe to live here, they tell us. It's unwise to start a business or bring a family. No man in his right mind would invest capital in Arizona Territory, they say. Well, I'm afraid it's true. Don't you think it is?"

"I'm afraid it might be," the judge said.

The governor nodded. "Shipping and mining and the cattle industry are losing tens of thousands to banditry—monthly. The number of killings in Arizona is reaching scandalous proportions. In the past six months half a dozen of our best peace officers have been shot down in cold blood. Mr. Ives and Col. Randolph and I decided some time ago that if we didn't take some decisive action, we would have a repetition of the tragedy of eighteen years ago, when the Earps were chased out of the Territory and bands of badmen practically ran the whole region."

Governor Murphy paused, as though for emphasis, and continued: "Most of us have been battling for Arizona statehood for some years. Now, I can say as a plain fact that we'll never reach that goal if we don't do something by way of making the Territory acceptable to the East. The East is where money and population come from—that's obvious. We're not civilized out here, you know, and at the moment we're doing damned little to build a civilization. The southern valleys of the Territory are highways for cattle thieves who rustle cattle in Mexico and sell them here, and rustle them here and sell them in Mexico. We're crowded with killers and runaway toughs from every other part of the country. The Apaches ravaged Arizona twenty years ago and since then nothing's changed—the toughs are still at it. If we want law we've got to fight for it."

"I agree," Judge Williams said, and added, "I know all this, Governor." He spoke gently.

"Of course. But I wanted you to think about it, specifically and urgently." The governor went right on talking. Judge Williams's eyes were half closed and he listened to the governor's continuing drone with only a part of his mind. He thought of the Territory's growth as he had seen it. The governor was anxious to see it change overnight, and that was good; there had to be some like him, or the civilization that he called for would never arrive. But the birth-pains of justice, the wrenching of order from the savage country, the introduction of law and human cultivation into a population thinly distributed over a hundred thousand square miles of desert and mountain vastness—these required time. It wasn't possible to instill a conscience in the frontier society overnight. Judge Williams had seen too much of life before his bench in Bisbee to think otherwise. And meanwhile, he thought, there seemed only one practical answer—the slow process of arbitration by the quick power of violence, by gun and rope.

The governor was speaking of possible futures, of the present and its fears, of the past and its lessons. The governor went on; Judge Williams thought the romance of these times was the romance of a land in time of peace at war within itself, in a strange kind of civil war rising out of the anarchy of the wilderness frontier. It had to be gentled, not conquered; yet no means but force was available. *Does that make sense?* Perhaps not. The gentility of the time was the gentility of people who clustered fearfully in the towns and in the manner of an ostrich refused to accept their primitive surroundings. The heroism of the time wasn't the brash recklessness of those who faced up to quick violent deaths, but the colder, quieter courage of the ones who faced it with a plow or a gingham dress and with moral conviction that history was being accomplished before their eyes and that they should act in such a way as to give it meaning.

The governor's voice came slowly, dimly into his mind: "And we've got to recognize the problem with our peace officers, too. Most of them close their eyes to a lot of evils.

Nine times out of ten they ignore wanted men in their bailiwicks, generally because the wanted men haven't committed local crimes. Even our honest officers are hampered by town limits and county lines, and a public apathy that terrifies me."

"The situation," Judge Williams said, "is bad. I presume you have an answer to it—that's why you called us here."

"Texas has Rangers," the governor said bluntly, and swept the three men with his glance. "So do we, now."

The judge's eyebrows lifted. "What?"

"The plan was worked out by Mr. Ives and Col. Randolph and myself."

"What have I to do with it, then?"

"Because you live in Bisbee, which is where the Rangers will have their headquarters," the governor said. "And because I trust you, old friend. And for one other reason."

"What's that?"

"We have chosen as the first captain of the Rangers an old friend of yours. Burt Mossman."

Judge Williams pursed his lips. "Well," he said, and nodded. "Well."

"Exactly," purred the governor. "Burt will need your cooperation, Starr. But that was not the specific reason for my calling this meeting. You see, a few days ago we pushed the bill through the Legislature creating the Rangers. The Legislature, as you know, consists of a number of skinflints, and all they've allotted us is enough of a fund to staff the Rangers with twelve men."

"Twelve?"

Governor Murphy nodded. "I know Burt Mossman well. I think he can do it. What we need is a solid body of men —capable, loyal, and intelligent."

"And tougher than anybody since Samson," the judge said. "I don't believe it will work, Governor."

"One step at a time," the governor said. "It will be a start. Burt Mossman has chosen as his lieutenant your Bisbee marshal, Dayton Graham. With a few more men of that caliber, the Rangers should start showing results soon. But that still isn't my real purpose today, Starr."

The governor paused. His expression was intense; he stood behind his own chair with his fists closed over its back. He said: "I've received an unconfirmed report that Mossman and three of his men have ridden into Mexico after a gang of thieves."

A hush fell on the room; in fairness the judge had to call it a hush. He stared at the governor. "But he can't do that. What's he trying to do, ruin our relations with Mexico?"

"Whether or not it can be done is beside the point. He may have done it already."

"We didn't bargain for this," Colonel Randolph interjected.

The governor watched Judge Williams. "This incident may cause a furor, Starr. We'll need your support."

"How can I condone an action like this? It's patently illegal—it violates every treaty between Diaz and the United States—it could cause all kinds of trouble."

"We're fighting for something bigger than a few hurt Mexican feelings," Governor Murphy said. His face thrust forward with a look of vision, a vision of pride. "Statehood has to come, Starr. If we stay as we are—which we can't, of course; we'll only slide back—but if we stay as we are, we'll never be able to bring in capital. Capital, gentlemen, is the bloodstream of a growing country. Without it we'll wither. Now, if this incident causes the Rangers to be disbanded, we'll be in a worse position than we were before. One small incident like this can wreck years of progress."

"Burt should have thought of that before he crossed the line into Mexico," said Colonel Randolph.

The governor gave his desk top a moment's attention. Then he put his hands on it, stiffened his elbows and sat down. "Gentlemen, don't ever repeat this—I'll call you all liars if I have to."

Ives, who had remained silent all this time, put his wise politician's eyes on the governor and said, "Go on."

"I gave Mossman full rein. I told him to cross the Border if he had to."

The judge's head lifted sharply. "You did what?"

"He had my permission—my orders, if you prefer. I must, in this privacy among us, accept responsibility for it."

"And," the judge retorted, "you must accept the irresponsibility of it."

"No. It had to be done. It would have accomplished only half our task if we left it possible for the toughs to walk across the Border into northern Mexico and conduct their raids from safety there. No place within a thousand miles of this Territory must remain safe for these outlaws. It has to be that way, gentlemen—can't you see it?"

No one spoke; no one moved. Governor Murphy said: "It may set your minds somewhat more at ease to know I've arranged, secretly of course, with the chief of the Northern Rurales for cooperation."

Colonel Randolph said, "Kosterlitzky?"

"Yes."

"I don't like him," Randolph said.

"He's ruthless, but he's efficient, and, I expect, reasonably honest."

Over at the side of the room, Ives was shaking his head back and forth. "Kosterlitzky and Burt Mossman are cut from the same cloth."

"Changing sides so quickly, are you?" the governor said.

"Well," Ives said, "it's fine in theory, Governor, and you know I supported it all the way, but there are a couple of things against it. As the judge said, it isn't legal, and you've done it behind the backs of higher authorities. Second, put the shoe on the other foot. What would our own people say, or think, or do, if a squad of Rurales came swarming into Arizona on the trail of Mexican criminals who'd escaped into our zone?"

"That's a chance we must take," the governor said.

"I'm sorry I mixed in this," Ives said bitterly.

"Why?"

"I don't trust Burt Mossman," Ives said. "This proves I was right."

"Rubbish," the governor said. "He's as honest as any man I've ever met."

"I didn't say he was dishonest," Ives said.

"What, then?"

Ives shook his head again. "It's hard to explain. Maybe it's his zeal."

"What's wrong with zeal? You've got plenty of it, I've noticed."

"I suppose I do," Ives muttered, and smiled faintly. "But it's not the same kind."

"What are you driving at?"

Ives frowned in a puzzled way. "Maybe it's this—maybe Mossman hasn't got any social conscience. He's tough, but

I don't think he's as tough as he likes to pretend he is. I don't think any man alive is that tough. He likes to give the impression that he's never needed anybody and he never will. I just won't buy it—he's too damned independent. He's interested in nothing but himself—he's a self-centered and self-sufficient man. Governor, Burt Mossman is a friend of mine but I don't think he really gives a damn about Arizona Territory. He respects you and he respects Colonel Randolph here, and that's why he agreed to take this job. But he doesn't really give a damn about any living human being other than himself. And that's why I distrust him, if you've got to know."

Governor Murphy shook his head and spoke in a very soft, very mild tone, "I think you're missing the whole point, my friend."

"Perhaps I am, then. What is it?"

The governor's lips made a small upturn; he said, "It's Burt's self-interest that makes him particularly valuable to us."

Judge Williams's forehead had been gathering into ripples all the while. Now he said, "I don't follow that."

The governor touched his sideburns, and dropped his hands on the desk. "Burt's selfishness isn't a material kind of selfishness. I admit he's self-centered. I admit he shows no pity. I admit he's ruthless. I admit he's prone to snap judgments and unwilling to admit mistakes—but then, I've never seen him make a mistake of any significance. I admit that by most standards he's proud and even vain at times. But it's my belief that these parts of him make him an asset to us."

"I haven't even begun to understand that," Ives said, and the judge nodded in agreement. Near the door, Colonel Randolph just sat smiling vaguely, listening to the governor talk.

"We'll all agree that Burt's an honest man, won't we?" the governor said, and when no one argued, he said, "All right—couple his honesty with his pride, then—what do you get?"

"You'll have to tell us," Ives said.

"You get Burt Mossman's breed of man," the governor said. "He's totally concerned with his own actions but he's not concerned in a cheap way—he's not interested in making an impression on anybody or making a quick profit or pleasing the Divinity so he can get a comfortable berth in the hereafter. He's not interested in his own comfort or even his own happiness—he's only interested in justifying himself *to himself*. We all have to answer to someone. Burt Mossman has to answer to himself—and that's the hardest of all. That's why he's concerned with doing the best he can—and that's why I trust him implicitly to handle the job he's taken. He's never compromised on any point in his life."

"Exactly," Ives said quickly. "But a man in his present position has to know when to make compromises."

"Maybe—maybe," Governor Murphy said. "We've always gone under that theory. But it might be wrong."

"You've made many a compromise," Ives said pointedly.

"I suppose I have," the governor replied. "I'm interested in my own career and in the future of Arizona. I mean to employ every means available to further both of those causes. Burt Mossman is an excellent means."

"But he has no interest in the progress of Arizona," Ives objected.

"Who's to say? He has an interest in it if his job calls for such an interest; and his job does call for it. Gentlemen, we all know what a back-scratching, finicky body the Legislature is. If we want to see order in this Territory, we have got to make a few sacrifices. Mr. Ives, I'm going to ask you to defend my Rangers to the last ditch in the Legislature. Colonel Randolph, I want you to exercise every control you have over the railroad and shipping lobbies. Judge Williams, you're to cooperate with Mossman and his Rangers to the extent of your ability. I want no questions, gentlemen; that's all."

CHAPTER III

BISBEE TOWN

Twenty years before, when Bisbee was just organizing itself, the town fathers had passed the first regulations. First among the ordinances they passed was the law stating that women were not to be allowed to work in saloons or gambling halls within the town limits.

But that didn't prevent Ellen Drury from running the town's most popular roulette game. Her table was set up nightly just beside the front door of Jim Letson's Turf Saloon. Ellen used no magic charm; her game was honest. She was popular because she was probably the prettiest unattached woman in Bisbee; she was successful because she knew how to be aloof and at the same time how to be graceful.

BISBEE TOWN

The night was slow for business and Ellen was ready to close her game at one o'clock. Lamps glowed yellow around the walls of the room and the crowd was middling thin. Ellen called numbers, spun the wheel, tossed the little steel ball and raked chips across the green felt. Her shoulders lifted and dropped, partly with resignation. While she worked, she let her glance sweep the room, pausing on faces here and there, making her guesses at the types of men hidden behind those faces.

Flesh broiled red, big hands and copper dust on his clothes—that one was a Finn, a miner from one of the shafts nearby. The one beside him would be a shift foreman or gang man: he too had the look of hard work, but he wore like a crown the air of authority, of power over men. On down the bar, by himself, stood a short man, heavily constructed like a workman, but whose skin was pale and whose palms were plainly smooth. That man, a stranger, wore the card-playing man's trademark: a silver brocade vest under his broadcloth short-coat. Two or three of those farther down the bar were gentlemen of the town. She knew them vaguely, storekeepers and clerks. They had the stamp of the town as plainly as a farm boy had the walk of the plow. A few cowboys rustled quietly around the room, their spurs clinking and their laughter coming quick and easy. Ellen felt acutely alone just then; the saloon passed her by, with its loneliness bred of physical closeness without familiarity. But her face remained a noncommittal pretty mask, long and clear-featured with wide-spread green eyes that tilted at the corners. Her hair was the color of pale sand. She closed her eyes and opened them; she said, "That's all tonight, boys," and paid off the last winners. Then she folded the felt strip and put it in ʰthe wheel, and spent ten minutes making neat piles of chips, which she took back to the cashier. The cashier said, "Good night tonight?" And Ellen answered, "So-so. I'll see you tomorrow."

She went forward along the bar toward the door. An arm reached out, arresting her, and she turned to look into the pale face of the man she had noted before, the stranger in gambler's clothes. That man smiled with a glisten of teeth and said, "Allow me to buy you a drink."

"Thank you, no." She touched his arm and pushed it away; she saw the smile leave his face, and she went on past him through the crowd, which opened to make a path for her. Someone shouted, " 'Night, Ellen!" and she lifted her hand and waved, not having seen who had called to her. Outside, she turned on the wooden sidewalk and went toward the Plaza's center, where O.K. Street and Brewery Gulch intersected with Main Street. Yellow street lamps made little pools of light along the walks. Very few people were abroad at this hour. A crowd of horsemen, three or four, came up the Naco Road from the bottom of the Warren District, passed the Copper Queen's smelter and the Old Customhouse, and rode past Ellen with a small flurry of powder dust. Sight of those men arrested her and she paused, hesitant; presently she turned on her heel, gathering her wrap about her shoulders, and went back up the Plaza toward the post office, where the four men were dismounting.

Two of the men had walked directly up the stairs and inside; the other two remained below the steps momentarily, talking. One was Dayton Graham; the other was Burt Mossman. It was sight of Mossman that had changed the direction of Ellen's steps and quickened her pace. But by the time she had gone around the horses and come up to the stairway, Mossman was already inside the building and the only figure remaining in the night was Dayton Graham. Above her head a window flashed alight and spread a cone of illumination out over the Plaza. Dayton Graham, who was no longer Bisbee's marshal, saw her coming forward and waited where he was until she was close, whereupon he said, "No, we didn't catch them."

"Why did you give up so quickly?"

"There'll be another day," Graham said. "Nobody could find them in those hills down there. Kosterlitzky's got a whole company of Rurales out looking for them, but he won't find them."

"But you will?"

"Cap will," Graham said, and looked at Ellen more sharply. "You didn't come over here to talk to me," he said.

"You're a sly fox, Graham."

He smiled. "That's why I'm still alive."

"Why did you quit your job?" she said.

"To take a better one."

"He doesn't pay you as much."

"No," Graham said. He seemed to let the conversation die willingly, but the girl revived it:

"What drives him?"

The ex-marshal shook his head. "I'm his lieutenant now, Ellen. Don't ask me to pry into his secrets."

"Then," she said quickly, "I'll pry into yours. Why do you want to work with him?"

Graham considered her over a stretching interval through the half-light; his face turned so that light reflected frostily from his eyes and his frame seemed even taller than it was. "Don't play for him," Graham said. "It will only bring you grief, Ellen. He's probably the only man alive that you couldn't get by lifting a finger."

"I couldn't get you," she suggested.

"No," he admitted, and laughed. "But I'm a family man. That's different."

"I suppose so," she said, not certainly. "I've never talked to him. Did you know that?"

"You don't have to talk to him. All you need is a good look."

"Yes," she said. "What is he, Graham?"

"Why," Graham said, "he's a man, Ellen. Damn few men in this world. Now you listen to me—don't set your sights on him. All you can do is lose."

"Maybe," she breathed. "You'd better go on inside, Graham."

"What?"

"You're a family man. Let's not have anyone see you talking to me in the middle of the night."

He laughed. "That won't trouble my wife."

"There's no point in stirring up gossip," she said. "Gossip's just as bad whether it's true or not."

"Well," he answered, "I thank you for your thoughtfulness, lady, but I can handle my own battles, with toughs or with wagging tongues." But just the same he tipped his hat to her and wheeled slowly, climbing the stairs to the post office door and pushing inside. Ellen smiled a little smile, faraway and bittersweet, and tightened her wrap a little against the chill before she went across the Plaza and took a post, standing in the deep shadows by John Angius's grocery store; she faded into the darkness and became no more than one motionless shadow among many.

She was still in that exact position forty minutes later when the post office door opened and two men came down the steps. One was Burt Mossman; the other was a very tall, very young man, who listened to Mossman's quiet speech with his head dipped down in earnest attentiveness. She heard Mossman's soft words echoing distantly across the silent Plaza: "Get some sleep, Santee. We'll be in the saddle by sunup."

The tall young man nodded and took the reins of his horse, and turned to lead the horse away toward the O.K. Stable. Thereupon the girl stepped into the dim paleness of the dusty Plaza and crossed toward the post office, where Mossman stood with his head bowed thoughtfully. Her shoes scratched the dust a little; Mossman's hat brim rose, indicating his interest, and he stayed like that, watching her, while she advanced and stopped a yard away from him, saying, "I'm Ellen Drury."

He made no answer of any kind; he stood watching her, studying her. She tried to interpret his expression but she could find nothing in it beyond polite interest. He did not seem confused; he was not angry; he was not amused; she saw no hungers in his glance. The quarter-moon washed his face with a little glow, softening the lines of his features. He was, she judged, about thirty-two or thirty-three, though it was hard to tell in the light. He was no taller than she, yet she felt that she was looking upward when she watched him. She said to him, "You've never come to play at my table."

"I don't play roulette," he answered; his voice was even, courteous.

"But you know who I am."

"Of course," he said with a slight bow of his head. She

found no irony in it. He said, "Did you wish something?"

She folded her arms, pulling the wrap around her shoulders tighter, and wondered whether he was really watching her face at all; she had an impulse to turn around, to see if there were something behind her he was looking at, but he wasn't, and she didn't turn—it was just the way he had of using his eyes. She said, "Yes, I wanted something."

He stood with his arms hanging straight, his legs spread a few inches, his back quite straight in the military manner assumed by many short men. Ellen said, "I wanted to meet you."

"Now we've met." His answer was short but not curt; nonetheless it disappointed her, possibly because he had shown no interest whatever. His glance was steady and mild. He said: "It's a late hour. Are you going home?"

She was about to say no, she wasn't; then she lifted her head and met his eyes and said, "Yes."

His eyebrows lifted, almost imperceptibly, and she said, "Up Tombstone Canyon a few blocks."

He might have been surprised but he didn't show it. Tombstone Canyon was not Bisbee's crib district; rather, it was the location of the town's finest houses. Mossman stepped to the outside of the walk and turned, lifting his elbow a little; she put her hand on it and matched his steps, going uphill toward Tombstone Canyon. They walked silently for a brief while. She caught the faint scent of saddle leather on his clothes, which were rugged but well cut of good cloth. His coat was buckskin, his trousers broadcloth, and he wore a large revolver at the left on his waist. Ellen said abruptly, "I hadn't expected this gallantry of you."

"What had you expected?"

"I don't know." She felt the strength in him; it was implied by the way he held his arm, relaxed but strong. She said, "I've seen you come and go."

"Yes."

"You were in business here before you became an officer."

"Briefly. The meat-packing business."

"Where did you come from before that?"

"Hashknife," he said, and it made her think of endless square miles of lush grass, herds of cattle in the thousands. She had once ridden the Santa Fe train across Hashknife —hours of Hashknife, at fifty miles an hour. She said, "You worked there?"

"I was the manager."

"I see," she said. "I didn't know you were a cattleman."

He didn't answer her; presently she said, "Do you mind my questions?"

His face turned. Upward to the west was Quality Hill; they had passed the road leading up to the Copper Queen's Glory Hole. He said, "No, I don't mind," but she felt that his reason for not minding was that her talk was not reaching him; it made her feel lonely, as she had felt in the saloon. But no expression crossed her face. She said: "Why did you give up the meat-packing business? Did you lose money?"

"I made money."

"Then why?"

He shrugged. It was all the reply she got. Presently she said, "Up this path," and turned off the road to the right. They passed two large homes belonging to engineers from the East, and the home of Charles Clawson, who was the superintendent of the Copper Queen enterprises of Phelps Dodge Consolidated. Up here, in the steep section of Tombstone Canyon, the houses clung to the slopes above one another. She had often heard miners' talk of how "You can sit on one front porch and spit in the next fellow's chimney." Stairs of wood and stone went up the hillside; casual dirt trails wound around among rocks and occasional trees and presently, at the top of the hill overlooking the top of Mule Pass Gulch, Ellen said, "Here."

Looking down the Gulch, Bisbee was visible as far as the bend beyond Brewery Gulch. Above on the summit sat a long wooden house with a galleried porch and half a dozen planted shade trees. She saw Mossman's eyelids open a little wider and close down again. He said, "This is yours."

"Yes. I'm a businesswoman."

"I see that," he said in a tone that was at once cool but not unfriendly. He stepped back from her at the edge of the porch, tipping his hat, starting to turn; she said, "Wait."

He stood fast, saying nothing. Her eyes dropped away from his face. A rock ground under her shoe; she kicked it away. The precious strip of lawn was a dark carpet on both sides of the path. She said, "Would you like a cup of coffee?"

He did not answer immediately; she grew impatient and moved, and he said: "Yes. Thank you."

She lit a lantern by the door and carried it inside. When Mossman had closed the door behind him he said, "Perhaps this isn't wise."

"You're the only man I've ever allowed in this house alone with me," she said.

"Honored." There was no trace of sarcasm in his voice.

She went around the drawing room lighting lamps and then left the room long enough to set a pot of water on the stove and light the fire. When she returned, Mossman was standing by the front window, holding the curtain aside with one hand, looking out toward Bisbee and the smaller camps in the pass below.

She said, "Sit down." He moved to a chair with quiet obedience. She took a seat nearby and talked quietly. "What are you?"

Something in the depth of his glance reached out and crossed the space between them. Mossman said: "I'm a cattleman. I'm a meat-packer. I'm a manhunter. I'm a businessman. I've built an opera house; I'm a killer." He moved in his seat. "Is that an answer?"

"No."

He smiled. "No. Not to you. To most men it would be—and to most women."

"We're not most men and women," she answered. "What's the reason for a man like you?"

"I am the reason."

"Then that's the meaning?"

He nodded. "I am the meaning." Something glittered in his eyes; it might have been triumph.

"But you're lonely."

"No," he said, "I'm not."

"Then it's unhappiness I see."

"I'm not interested in happiness."

She shook her head. "I don't understand you."

"Is that why you brought me up here?"

"Yes," she said. "Most men are made of glass. I see all of them at once, immediately. But there's an iron shield in front of you—I don't see anything."

"Why must you find out?"

"I don't like what I see in glass men," she said. "Don't you see the same things?"

"Yes, I see them."

"You don't like them either, do you?"

"I've never given it much thought," he said mildly. His face, she reflected, looked like the face of an arrogant and powerful man; but the face meant nothing, it was the eyes that told of a man's soul, and Mossman's eyes were guarded at all times. She said, "You don't think of them, do you?"

"Who?"

"Anyone."

"Not a great deal," he said. "I have to know them well enough to do my job properly. Beyond that I have no interest in anyone."

"What do you have interest in?"

"My job."

She shook her head; she thought she understood him, yet she was not sure. She went out of the room to pour coffee, and soon returned, handing him a mug and returning to her own chair with her coffee. She said: "You didn't have to come here with me. Why did you?"

His answer was not in words. It was in the steadiness, even in the blankness of the way his eyes held hers. It was a definite answer, in a way. She said, "Dayton Graham told me not to talk to you."

"Perhaps he was right."

"I don't think so. I think I can break your shield."

"You can't," he told her. "Why do you want to try?"

"I want to know what's behind the shield."

"I am."

"I know. But who are you?"

"I've told you that," he said. He sipped off the top of the coffee and she thought he was the most enigmatic man she had ever known; yet he was no enigma at all; he was the one person she had met who was most like her. Yet his self-sufficiency was so much more complete than hers that she felt frightened enough to say, "Do you think I'm beautiful?"

"Yes." He put his cup down on a table beside him. "I think you're beautiful."

"You're the only man who's ever said that to me without making me feel insulted."

He smiled a little. "Perhaps that's because you know I'm telling you the truth."

"Yes. You'd never flatter me."

"I'd never flatter anyone."

She nodded. "I'd give my soul to be as sure of myself as you are of yourself."

"You wouldn't give your soul for anything," he answered. "Most people give up their souls all the time. It's easy to do. The hard thing is to keep your soul—not to let it mix with anyone else's."

"You mean not to let public opinion dictate my life?"

"Something like that," he said. "It's not a question of dictating, though."

"Then you mean the hard thing is to ignore it."

"Not exactly. To ignore something, you've got to know it's there."

"But you don't know it's there."

"Not often."

She shook her head. "You confuse the hell out of me, Mossman."

"Then," he said, standing up, "I've made a mistake coming here. Good night."

"No. Wait. Sit down." She knew there was a little urgency in her tone, but she didn't want to conceal anything from him; it would be the gravest possible wrong to make any pretenses before him.

Mossman did not sit down. He looked around the big drawing room, at its plentiful but not crowded furniture, and touched the points of his mustache with his forefinger, one at a time. He said, "Do you need this place?"

"I needed it before. No one comes here. But I did need it, yes. I don't need it tonight."

"What do you need tonight?"

"Nothing," she said.

"Not this house."

"No."

"Nor your wealth."

"No."

"Do you need me?"

He was watching her. She said, "No."

He only stood watching her over the broken interval; she said, "Then you'll stay?" And he did not move. She frowned angrily; she said, "Damn you, Mossman! What do you want of me?"

"If you ever do anything intended to please me," he said, and trailed off, not with uncertainty but with a plain meaning.

"I understand," she said. "I won't try to anticipate what you want of me—I won't try to be whatever you want me to be."

"Just so," he murmured. He sat down and picked up his coffee.

CHAPTER IV

"AND THE FOURTH HORSEMAN WAS DEATH"

There were four riding north at dawn: Santee rode at the rear, beside Ranger Bill Maxwell, and ahead of them were the jogging backs of Mossman and Carlos Tafolla, who was a Ranger from St. Johns with a reputation for being tough enough to be tougher than the next man, no matter who the next man was.

"I get the feeling," Mossman had said, "Chacon will be on his way to the White River country northeast of here. I want to cut him off before he gets that far. We haven't enough of a crew here to put up a fight against that whole crowd of toughs that headquarter up there. You rode with Creed Jacks, Santee—any ideas?"

"If Creed was leadin' the bunch," Santee had said, "they'd camp at Satterlee's old line cabin on the forks of the White, the night before they rode into camp. But that's just what Creed would do. I can't speak for Chacon."

"Then we'll take the train as far as Safford, and ride up from there."

They took the Southern Pacific and spent part of the day in stock cars; they unloaded the horses at Safford and pressed north over the Gila Mountains and the Black River through jaggedly rugged country cut by steep cross-canyons and sudden buttes.

At the base of the sawtooth risings of one timber-clad slope they came upon fresh sign of five horses and a pack mule, tracks coming in from the south and turning north-east along the White River canyon trough. Santee said: "We've hit a piece of luck. But where's that sixth man?" And remounted his horse.

"Come on."

The four horsemen drummed along the river valley, now and then halting to read sign. In the late afternoon the tracks split away from the river and entered a patch of rocks, crossing a black-scarred burn, slowing down the trackers; Santee said: "Shortcut over the pass to the forks. They're only five hours ahead of us at the most—look where the wind hasn't blown over those tracks."

Rubbed spots in the bridle metal sent flashes against his eyes. He pushed his hat forward over his face and, when he looked that way, he saw the blank darkness of Mossman's expression, the heavy roll of his lips under the hang of his mustache. Before them the violent pattern of the land buckled up in ascending crooked tangles. Mossman's shuttered eyes kept constant watch on all of it.

He said, to no one in particular, "That missing sixth horse will be Chacon—too smart to run with the pack."

"I hope you're wrong, Cap," said Bill Maxwell.

"No," Mossman said definitely. Santee watched his eyes, which were never really open, never really shut; crow's-feet surrounded the corners. It was a question to Santee whether Mossman was as tough as the armor of his cheeks made his seem.

"In a little while," Carlos Tafolla muttered, "we will have some fun, *amigos*." But the smoothness of his suggestion fooled no one. There was a huskiness in his voice.

On the nearby horizon-swells Santee saw nothing more than greasewood and the spindle tracery of yucca stalks and ocotillo and, down in sheltered pockets where there was water, the heavier green of sycamore and cottonwood. Santee heard Carlos Tafolla's quiet talk cut across the air, "I feel a hand on my shoulder."

Santee said, "What?"

"My wife, in St. Johns," Tafolla said, and stopped. Then his mouth opened and he laughed. "I must have got the spooks," he said; his laughter rose. Tafolla's eyes were wide and bright with the laughter; his humor bubbled and Santee could not look at him without smiling in answer.

Sweat rolled out of his pores. The sun slapped hard on the earth, pressing down heavy layers of sluggishly stirring dust. They dropped along the side of a hill and clattered through a short, high-sided defile; then the walls fell back and they broke out of the canyon mouth onto a short flat, glistening with mica bits in the ground and in the rocks. Slivers of brilliance danced against Santee's eyes. They thundered around the end of a tangled grove of paloverde, raising strong echoes among the rocks, and put their horses upslope across a rising open covered with white-streaked boulders. Behind them, in the south, a wall of dark clouds boiled forward, promising bad weather.

"Santee," Mossman said.

"What?"

"If Chacon's with that crew, keep close watch—don't even wink."

"Why," Santee said, "I watch everybody. I guess you learn that."

"Learn it or die." Then Mossman produced a pair of his chunky cigars, without which Santee had never seen him, and offered one. Santee accepted it and nipped off the end. He chuckled. "There was a time when you wore out a lot of Hashknife grass tryin' to run me down."

"You were smart," Mossman said, without expression. "Smart enough to quit."

"I had my fun. I never hurt anybody. I didn't want to start."

"Santee," Mossman said, "listen to me."

"All right."

"You're on the other side of the fence now. Don't swap back."

"I didn't have it in mind."

"I know." There was gentleness in Mossman's voice.

"I thought you didn't give a damn about anybody?"

Mossman said nothing. His glance was all the time impersonally surveying the rock-strewn hillsides. "We can't talk law-book justice to a crew of toughs who outnumber us a hundred to one. Our job's to fight a war. Understand this, Santee—I give you free rein and I ask no questions. Times will come when you'll have to use your rifle first and your warrant afterward. Times will come when you won't even have a warrant."

Mossman's head turned and he looked directly at Santee. "When those times come a bullet will have to do."

Santee said, "No warrants—no questions. You're giving us a license to shoot anybody we feel like shooting."

"We can't afford to turn the other cheek," Mossman answered, "we haven't enough cheeks."

Something—perhaps it was a stoutly contained anger—seemed about to break through the noncommittal brightness of Mossman's eyes; but then he turned his face to look away forward. Santee thought: *What happened to him? That woman he met last night? I've seen her dealing roulette.* He didn't understand. Mossman was a tense, square shape in the saddle; his steady eyes watched everything. He said, "It's my belief that the meek will only inherit this part of the earth if the strong are here to protect them." His words sprawled softly and easily, without force; but Santee felt the powerful wash of feeling behind them, enough to answer:

"Since when do you care about the meek?"

Mossman said, "I don't. My job is to protect them."

During that pink-clouded hour between day and night, the bank of clouds rushed forward with great haste. At eleven o'clock, with blackness thick around them, the four horsemen topped a minor mountain chain and swung downward through a pass on the northern shed; and by an hour after midnight, the drizzle of soft rain began to descend upon them. Santee unstrapped his oilskin poncho from the saddle cantle and put his head through the hole in its center. He said: "This will wash out their tracks in another hour. We'll just have to hope they're holed up where we think they are."

Dawn was close upon them before they rode down to the bank of the White near the forks and turned upriver at a trot. "Easy," Santee said. "Just around the bend, now."

Through a few cloud-slits in the east, the sky emitted enough dawn-light to perceive the rectangular darkness of a cabin near the river edge. Mossman held up his right hand and halted his horse, and drew from his saddlebag an army telescope, through which he examined the camp.

"Five horses," Mossman said. "One mule. Saddled and ready to go." He folded the 'scope and put it away.

They sat their horses within two hundred yards of open ground of the cabin. Santee thought back. These men ahead in the cabin—how long had it been since they had held up the hardware store in Bisbee? Two days? Three? Mossman stepped down and handed to Santee the reins of his horse. "This trip," Mossman said, "you'll stay with the horses. If you hear gunshots, come on the run. If I whistle, then you're clear to walk in."

"Hell," Santee said. "Why not tie the horses and all of us go in?"

"We may need the horses fast."

"Then why not ride in?"

"Hoofbeats would give us away," Mossman said. "Listen, Ranger—you'll follow orders." Santee adjusted his jacket collar, turned up against the rain, and felt the cold slickness of the poncho against the back of his hand.

He stood by the head of his horse motionless and impatient while his three companions fanned out across the meadow, pressing forward quietly on foot, with the red dawn coming up dimly over the humps eastward, filtering through the cold bleakness of rain and cloud. Raindrops fell at a little slant, sweeping gently across the line of his sight.

"Watch out for Creed," Santee murmured, seeing Mossman advance with his gun up. "Watch Creed." Santee stepped back to the flank of his horse and drew his rifle from the saddle boot, and waited that way while the slow attack continued. Gray light grew slowly brighter. Santee was sure someone inside that cabin would spot the Rangers moving in across the open ground; but time stretched and there was no alarm. The steady pour of rain made the air musky and the cabin hard to see in spite of the growing light. Water fell in large drops from the trough of his hat brim, dropping past the tip of his nose. Behind him the river gurgled and swept away down the bend.

Finally the three men drew close to the door. Santee's grip tightened around the rifle. He saw one of them—it might have been Carlos Tafolla but the light was poor—post himself outside the door while one of the others raised his boot and kicked the door in. Then all of them charged into the cabin.

Immediately he heard a single shot. Its echoes lifted and died. He saw two shadowy men leap from a side window and round the corner of the building to reach the horses. They were in their saddles and on the run before Santee had the sense to jump on his horse, yank the three sets of reins behind him and plunge forward.

The three horses behind him ran tangled among themselves, and by the time he reached the cabin the two escaping riders had disappeared beyond a farther rise of ground. The land was splashed with pale red illumination, dripping. Burt Mossman boiled out of the cabin and grabbed the three pairs of reins out of Santee's fist. As though it came to him against the rush of a great wind, Santee heard Mossman's distant shout:

"Get after them, boy!"

His ears pounded. The horse leaped under him from Mossman's slap. He wheeled and broke into a gallop across the river-bottom meadow. When he achieved the crest where the two fugitives had disappeared, Santee knew that his horse, punished by its long journey, would not be able to match the outlaws' fresher mounts. Disgusted, he halted atop the rise and scanned the broken country ahead.

The two horsemen seemed confused; they rode almost to the far end of a canyon and then suddenly changed course. He saw them cut back eastward into a side gully. It gave him a chance at them, and he spun off the rise, putting his horse across a hogback running northeast, hoping to intersect their trail. "That was Creed's roan," he said; his words rode away on the wind. While he ran on across the rough country with raindrops running down his back, he wondered what the single gunshot issuing from the cabin had meant. Was someone shot? Or had it just been a warning fired by one of the outlaws, giving the two in the back room a chance to escape?

He circled a grove of stunted pine. It was then that the horse stopped short. Below him was a steep talus slope; and, fifty yards to the left, the two fugitives were galloping toward him along the floor of the steep-sided ravine.

The two men had their attention pinned on what lay behind them, over their shoulders; they had not seen him.

"Creed," Santee said; he was breathing heavily. "Creed."

The two outlaws had their bodies hunched, their heads turned. Santee dismounted with his rifle, levered a cartridge into the chamber, and brought it up to his cheek. Then he hesitated, speaking softly again, "Creed."

They were almost directly below him when he called out:

"Hold it!"

They stopped in a swirl of clotted red clay; it settled quickly in the drizzle. Creed Jacks's head whipped around. Santee said, "Don't move a hair, Creed."

"Santee—God damn you!"

"Grab a cloud," Santee said, sounding tough, uncertain of what he should do next. He moved the rifle muzzle slightly toward Creed's head; he said: "One at a time, now —you first, Red. Unbuckle your gun belt with your left hand and let it fall."

He waited while Red obeyed sullenly. Creed spoke in a charged monotone: "You'll never make this stick. Ain't no man alive . . ."

"Now you, Creed," Santee said. Both men watched him in wide-eyed rage.

Creed, bearded and burly, still had his left hand on his reins. When he lifted that hand, the horse backed up a step, thus concealing Creed behind the body of his partner. Santee felt a sudden drop in his lungs; his hand turned white clutching the rifle, and he knew at once that Creed had reached for his gun. He knew one other thing too: he must be quick or die.

He dropped flat along the rim of the slope and sighted along the barrel. Abruptly he realized that Creed had fired his pistol once; he smelled powder and had a vague, unreal memory of hearing the report. Before him, Red was dragging his rifle from its scabbard under his knee; and still Santee hadn't touched the trigger. Something was wrong in him. He blinked; he felt his pulse jump and there were tears spoiling his vision; but he jerked the trigger, yanked the lever open and jacked it shut, and sighted along the barrel once more.

But his target was gone. Where Red had been he saw an empty saddle. He choked. All this had happened in a minute fraction of time, yet it seemed to move with deliberate, dreamlike slowness.

In falling, Red had knocked Creed askew on his saddle. That accident, Santee knew at once, was all that had saved his life. "God damn you, Santee!" Creed's call was a high wail; his pistol rose. Santee said through clenched teeth, "I've got to," while he put a bullet through the bridge of Creed's nose.

The rifle rocked against his shoulder. "I've got to—God! Creed?"

Creed threw up his arms; his head snapped back and he dropped from the saddle. Santee couldn't look at him. His glance shifted; he tried to find Red.

Red lay on the uneven ground, pressed against the ravine wall. Santee's bullet had gone down into his chest; bloody saliva foamed slowly at his lips. Santee's stomach turned and his eyes closed.

He knew he had to make sure. With an effort of will he slid down the slope's loose rockslide to stand on the floor of the lonely arroyo with his rifle ready. A trickle of water gurgled down the center of the gully, making an irregular stripe against the brick-red earth. Santee felt rain strike his hands. He heard a rifle fire a single shot in the distance; then a sustained fire began, echoing over the hills, and kept up for some time. Santee lifted his head, frowning. The firing died down. There was one ragged aftervolley and then stillness; he pressed his lips tight and looked down.

Both of the gunshot men lay motionless on the floor of the arroyo. He knelt beside Red. There was a film of blood over Red's open eyes. He wasn't breathing. Santee moved, stumbling across the rivulet to Creed.

Breath wheezed intermittently in and out of Creed's lungs. He looked at Santee and Santee became certain that Creed was trying to say something to him, but he couldn't make it out, and Creed died that way, unable to make himself understood. Santee moved a few steps away, his rifle dangling almost forgotten from his fist. His knees gave way slowly; he sank to a numb crouch and threw up into the trickle of flowing rainwater.

He did his best to maintain an air of collected gravity when he approached the line cabin, leading the two horses with his victims laid across their saddles. There was no promise of change in the weeping grayness overhead. The swelled rush of the White River was a round roar in the near distance. Dayton Graham's horse, just arrived, stood near the cabin. Three men stood outside the cabin door; a fourth lay in the shelter of the overhanging roof-edge, and another knelt by him. Back near the trees was another prone figure, but that one was plainly dead—one of the outlaws. The misty light was poor. Santee stepped down slowly, testing his knees, and looked first at the two men Bill Maxwell was holding at gunpoint. He recognized them vaguely as figures out of a different past: Daniels and Clubfoot Bill. His attention shifted to the dead man out by the trees, and then to the two shapes under the eaves.

The crouching man was Cap Mossman; the prone one was Ranger Carlos Tafolla. Santee hurried forward. Mossman looked up at him and gestured with his hand. Santee nodded and kept silent, looking down at Tafolla. Blood stained the front of Tafolla's water-soaked shirt and Mossman was just then peeling the shirt back; but Tafolla lifted one hand weakly and Santee heard his indistinct voice, "It is no good bothering, *amigo.*"

Mossman bent forward to look underneath the shirt at Tafolla's chest. When he squatted back, Santee saw his reluctant nod. The wounded Ranger said, "I'd like some water."

Santee turned on his heel and trotted to his horse for his canteen. Dayton Graham came around the corner of the cabin leading the pack mule, and stopped by Tafolla to kneel and speak a few words. Then Graham took a split-handled spade and walked out toward the trees, toward the dead outlaw lying in the rain.

Santee's glance briefly, angrily touched the two disarmed prisoners standing silently by the cabin wall. When he came back with the canteen, Mossman took it from his hand without looking up, removed the cap and tilted the canteen so that Tafolla could drink. Afterward, Tafolla's arm came up and he used the back of his hand to wipe his lips. His arm flopped back. "*Bueno,*" he said. "That's good."

Mossman said, "Do you want anything?"

"One thing." Tafolla's shoulder lifted and his face tightened with pain; he dug into his pocket and produced a small object which he handed to Mossman. "This is for my wife," he said. "In St. Johns—you know her."

"Yes."

"Give her that and give her my month's salary. It is all she will have." Tafolla's eyes looked up. "You will do this?"

"Yes," Mossman said. His fist opened and Santee looked at it. Lying in Mossman's open palm was a dented, twisted silver dollar. Mossman dropped it into the pocket of his vest. "Anything else, Ranger?"

"Why, I think that is about all, *amigo*. I wish I could see Clubfoot Bill hang."

"He'll hang," Mossman said. His manner was calm. "You're a good man, Ranger."

"I was. I am proud to have ridden with you, *amigo*. I suppose I will see you all sometime. *Amigo*—this hole, it does not hurt any more."

"That's good."

"No," Tafolla said. "It is not good. It means I am done. *Por Dios*, I am tired!" His eyes slid slowly shut.

After a while Santee uttered a single word, "Dead?"

"Not yet. Not for a while."

"Jesus," Santee said suddenly. He dropped to a crouch beside Mossman. "Was it Clubfoot Bill that did this?"

"Yes."

Santee's head turned and he looked at the two men whom Bill Maxwell was holding prisoner: Daniels and Clubfoot Bill. Clubfoot Bill was a medium-tall man with leather-brown skin crisscrossed by a mass of scars. He had a dour, hatchet-chinned face and a flattened nose; his hat was flop-brimmed and stained with sweat, his hands were smooth, his clothes were filthy. Clubfoot Bill gave Santee a single look that was utterly blank and returned his attention to the ground by his boots. Santee heard Mossman speak softly: "You know him. What's his tender point?"

"Don't know him that well," Santee murmured in answer. "But it would be a pleasure to find out."

"All right," Mossman said. He was regarding Tafolla with his customary enigmatic expression.

Santee looked at the edge of the trees, where Dayton Graham was busy digging a grave for the dead outlaw. Santee said, "Who's that?"

"Bill Smith."

"I don't know him."

"He robbed a train in Utah and a store in New Mexico."

"Tied in with Creed's bunch?"

"That's hard to say," Mossman said. "He was here— that's all we know." Mossman was watching Tafolla's face. Once he leaned forward to put his ear close to Tafolla's nose. When he straightened he said, "Not yet," and looked behind him at the two dead men Santee had brought in. "Who are those two?"

"Creed Jacks and Red Weaver. They didn't give me a choice."

Mossman's response was a grunt. Santee found no satisfaction and no triumph in Mossman's expression. Santee said, "How'd this happen to Tafolla?"

"After you left, Clubfoot Bill and Bill Smith made it out to the trees somehow. Tafolla and I went after them. We started shooting and after a while Smith called out that he wanted to surrender. We told him to throw down his guns and come out of the timber. He came. Clubfoot Bill was right behind him. What we didn't know was that they'd put their feet through the slings of their rifles. They were dragging the rifles along through the grass with their feet."

"And they opened up?"

Mossman nodded. "Tafolla stood up and called some orders. Smith pretended to trip, and went for his rifle. Clubfoot Bill got his gun going too and shot Tafolla before we had a chance to drop flat. Then I fired a few shots and by that time, Dayton Graham had worked up behind them. We had them boxed, but Smith didn't want to give up. It was Tafolla who killed him, before he passed out. That's all."

Santee nodded. "Then Chacon wasn't here at all."

"No."

"Maybe he's still in Mexico," Santee said.

"Maybe," Mossman said vaguely. He looked tired. "We'll have to bury Creed and Red. I saw another shovel inside."

"All right."

"Santee."

"What?"

Mossman said, "Three graves, Santee." All the while he was watching the shallow lift and fall of Tafolla's chest.

"Yes." Santee turned into the cabin. It was old and stuffy with the musty scent of disuse and wood rot. The oilpaper windows admitted little illumination; the floor was half an inch deep in dust, matted down by the day's gray moisture. Santee found the shovel, spade-handled and split along the wood, and took it outside.

It was the outlaw Daniels, standing in front of Ranger Maxwell's gun, who spoke up: "Santee—you're a jackleg traitor, you're a God-damned murderer. You knew Creed.

You knew Red—you used to ride with them. Those boys might have been a little wild but they wasn't bad, they wasn't killers . . ."

"Then they shouldn't have pulled guns on me," Santee said tautly. "I gave them a chance to surrender."

"Sure," Daniels said. Beside him, Clubfoot Bill was concentrating doggedly on the toes of his boots. A drop of water fell from one of the points of Daniels's mustache. "Sure you did. I wonder if Creed would back up your story, was he in any shape to argue."

Santee looked at Mossman. Kneeling beside Tafolla, Mossman hadn't taken his eyes off Santee.

Santee said, "All I can give you is my word."

"Your word's enough," Mossman said. But his tone was cool and he turned away, bending over Tafolla.

Daniels said: "How do you feel, Santee? How does a man feel when he shoots down his friend?"

"The law shot Creed down."

"You're the law, Santee."

"No," Santee said, "I'm not the law."

"Go ahead," Daniels jeered. "Hide behind the badge."

Santee picked up his canteen from the ground and put it away on his saddle. Standing by his horse, he leaned against the saddle with his arms over the top of it, his face down. Behind him he heard Ranger Bill Maxwell's voice, "Stand still, Daniels."

"Can't a man shift his feet? You damn Rangers are too cocky—one day you'll die, bucko."

"Why," Maxwell said, "I reckon I will, Daniels. I reckon all of us are dyin'. That's the difference between you and me. You just think about the dyin'—I think about what I ought to do before then, to make it right."

"What else I got to think about?"

"You might think about your sins," Maxwell said. "You might think about prayin'."

Santee heard a slow step and lifted his head. When he turned he saw Mossman standing by him. Mossman dropped to his haunches, stuck a cigar between his lips and whipped a match alight along the thigh of his trousers. He said in a drone, "Tafolla's dead."

Santee looked away, across the top of the saddle at the barren ground rising from the edges of the river valley. Over by the trees Dayton Graham was climbing out of the single grave he had dug for Bill Smith, the dead train-robber. Santee realized faintly that it had quit raining. The clouds were still dark and low. Mossman's quiet voice drifted up to him, "Getting it all straightened out, boy?"

"Not by a long shot."

"Maybe you never will."

Santee looked down. "Do you care?"

Mossman said nothing. Santee stepped away from the horse and glanced at the shovel he had left leaning by the cabin wall. Then he watched smoke rise in lazy spirals from the tip of Mossman's cigar. There was quiet wisdom in Mossman's voice and in the soft song of his voice. "You and I didn't sign on for pleasure."

"You're getting soft," Santee answered.

Mossman stood up. His cigar had grown a tall mottled ash, and he tapped it off gently. "Put those two fools to work digging graves," he said. "Then tell Maxwell and Dayton to come inside the cabin and get some sleep. You can guard these two for a few hours. Maxwell will relieve you." He touched Santee's shoulder. "Go on, boy."

The graves were finished. In a hollow tone Dayton Graham spoke a few words over each of them; he lingered over Carlos Tafolla's grave awhile, then followed Mossman and Bill Maxwell inside the cabin. Santee put the muzzle of his rifle on Daniels and Clubfoot Bill and took them down the field to the shelter of a thick cottonwood. The gray sky leaked a little moisture lethargically, not enough to be called rain. "Sit down," Santee said.

Daniels sat at the bole of the tree and proceeded to ignore Santee thereafter. Clubfoot Bill, scarred and ugly, sat down crosslegged, Indian-fashion, and pulled up a grass stalk which he stuck in his lips. Clubfoot Bill said, in a conversational, tentative tone, "Creed and Red was no good."

"I know," Santee said. Daniels did not move; if he was listening, he didn't show it.

"Old Creed was too ornery for my taste," Clubfoot Bill said.

"He ain't ornery now."

"Who's to say he ain't? I wonder about that." Unhappiness lay as a tightness around Clubfoot Bill's scarred, pushed-in face. His mouth corners sagged with a display of sour temper that no one could miss. After a while Clubfoot Bill said, "How come you to become a Ranger, Santee?"

"A job," Santee said. "I get paid. I eat."

"There's easier ways to come by money."

"This way's clean," Santee said.

"So?"

"I don't have to be looking down my backtrail," Santee said without vehemence.

"What you mean is, a man don't have to be scared so long as he's got an honest job."

"Something like that."

"But then, how come you joined up with Creed in the first place?"

Santee shrugged. "It looked easy."

"Why, hell, pilgrim—you didn't even have a decent excuse!"

"Who does? Did you?"

"You're damn right I did," Clubfoot Bill said. "I had my face."

"What of it?"

"You know what a man looks like when his horse steps into a gopher hole at dead gallop and flips him face-first into a cactus patch with a rock in the middle of it?"

"I reckon I do," Santee said, watching him.

"That's right." Clubfoot Bill's tone was ringed with bitterness. "You're lookin' at just such a man. That happened to me when I was fifteen. Took me six months to heal up and then my old man kicked me off the farm—he couldn't stand lookin' at me. I didn't have a damn thing against nobody. But I was ugly and I looked meaner than hell. I got a job and I got fired the next day. I drifted into El Paso and old John Selman took one look at me—he said anybody looked as mean as me just had to be mean. He threw me in the pokey. I got run out of Mesilla and Lordsburg and Tucson and Prescott. I rode into a cow camp and tried to steal a couple horses, but this damned foot tripped me up and I got caught. Happen it was Chacon's camp. His boys dragged me up to the fire and Chacon took one look at me and busted out laughin'. We been friends ever since."

"Chacon's nobody's friend," Santee said.

"Friend enough," Clubfoot Bill answered. "At least he didn't run me out or use me for a target."

"You trust him?"

"I never let him get behind me."

"Some friend you got," Santee observed.

Clubfoot Bill stiffened. "I can't pick and choose, Santee. I ain't got a fine-cut face like you. If I got one friend I'm lucky."

"If you're looking for sympathy from me," Santee said, "you won't find it. I remember Carlos Tafolla. That's his grave over there."

"He shot at me first."

"The hell he did."

"He did, damn it!"

"All right," Santee said mildly; then he said, "Where's Chacon?"

"In . . ." Clubfoot Bill began, and stopped. His lips distorted into a smile. "I may be ugly but I ain't that stupid, Santee. Chacon's where you won't ever find him until he wants to see you."

"We'll get him."

"Maybe—maybe."

"Hell," Santee said. "Shut up." But he had the feeling that tracking down Chacon would be a long, long hunt. He looked across the flats at the fresh-mounded graves; he looked at the saddled horses, and the dismal sky, and he wondered at the glimpses he had caught of chinks in Mossman's armor.

CHAPTER V

A MATTER OF PRIDE

Judge Starr Williams stood at the post-office door looking up toward Tombstone Canyon, watching the small group of horsemen swirl up the dusty grade finally to be absorbed by the distance. That was Mossman and his Rangers, taking the trail again. All summer long Mossman had spent not more than a day at a time in his office. He was always out in the hills horseback, most of the time alone, now and then with two or three other Rangers. Ostensibly Mossman's prey was usually someone who had recently broken the law, but the judge had the feeling these chases were only excuses Mossman used to justify cruising all over the Territory, on the chance of crossing Augustin Chacon's trail.

Mossman had brought in a dozen wanted men. He had hanged one outlaw summarily on the spot; he had caught up with Saliveras, Chacon's number two man, and blown Saliveras' head off with a rifle slug. His Rangers had dispersed across the valleys and mountains of Arizona, bringing down their men with cool, relentless efficiency; one had found his man in a Tucson saloon, and killed him there. Another had tracked his man into Mexico and brought him back, only to see the man released from custody because of the illegality of kidnapping a man out of Mexico; and on that occasion Judge Williams had seen a blaze of feeling cross Mossman's eyes, and go away. Dayton Graham had been shot by a saloon drunk, and when he had recovered from the wound Graham had sought out the drunk and killed him. The judge stood now before the long Bisbee post office and frowned deeply up the hill toward the point where Mossman had ridden out of sight; the judge was worried.

Fall's cool current of air swept the Plaza briskly, causing a chill to run up the judge's back. The first snows would come soon. He climbed the steps and returned to his office, picking a path through its littered disorder to his desk, where he sat and twirled a pencil between his fingers while he frowned vaguely at a printed form in front of him, not really looking at the form. The fire glowed deep red in the potbelly stove's isinglass window. The judge thought of Burt Mossman, and he thought of Governor Murphy's recent warning to him: *Mossman's getting out of hand, Starr. The Rangers are doing too good a job. Wiping the outlaws out to a man isn't the kind of cleanup we want. It's too final—it's too vicious.*

But Mossman wasn't a vicious man. The judge knew

that much about him; and this was what made him frown. He had told Mossman to bring his prisoners in for trial. Mossman had nodded and agreed with him; Mossman's eyes had glittered coolly. And the slaughter continued. The killings were always justified, in a strict and technical sense of legality; the Rangers always managed to make legitimate cases of self-defense out of their killings. But the judge knew the governor was right. As long as the Rangers remained ruthless and roughshod, they were breeding fear, and not respect, of the law.

It was Augustin Chacon who had flung his insolent challenge in Mossman's face in such a way that Mossman had commenced to trample the Territory in his obsessive vendetta. Augustin Chacon—*El Pelado*. Chacon was a tall and evilly handsome Indian with a square-chinned face and thin slices of eyes; Chacon affected crossed shoulder shell belts and a vast-brimmed sombrero in the manner of a Mexican revolutionary. And wherever Mossman rode, Chacon was just ahead of him, laughing at him. It had come to a point, Judge Williams felt, where the lesser outlaws, the wanted men whom Mossman's Rangers had captured by the scores and sometimes killed,—these lesser outlaws were only stepping-stones on the path that led to Augustin Chacon. And it should not be that way. Law was not a personal grudge-fight. Enforcement was not a feud. Burt Mossman was a friend of the judge's, and the judge had watched with pride the qualities of greatness in Mossman. But gradually the image of the laughing Chacon was destroying those qualities—and the judge was afraid.

He shook his head. He took his watch from the pocket of his vest and had a look at the time, and found himself hungry for lunch; he left his office and crossed the Plaza to the English Kitchen, and ate a thoughtful meal.

Afterward he stopped into the Turf Saloon to have a brief talk with Jim Letson, who owned the place. When he was about to leave, someone spoke to him, and he turned from the bar in time to see Ellen Drury lifting her hand to touch his sleeve. "I want to talk to you."

He touched his hat brim. "My pleasure," he murmured. "Come over to my office."

He offered her a chair in his office, and went around behind his desk; he lit a cigar and tilted his lean frame back in his seat and said, "What is it?"

"Burt Mossman," she said. Her tone was a little uncertain. "What's happening to him, Judge?"

Judge Williams watched her with interest. Instead of giving her a direct answer, he said, "Ellen, all the years you've lived in this town I've watched you preside over that roulette wheel and accumulate your fortune and never look twice at a single human being."

"You've watched all that?" she asked, with a quizzical turn to her lips.

"Every man watches you," he said softly, "for one reason or another."

She was sure of herself enough not to ask him to explain further. The judge noted that; and after a short hesitation he went on: "You've never shown the slightest interest in anyone. You've insulated yourself with that big house on top of the hill—you've let every miner's eyes slide off you and you've never cared whether they lingered. And now you ask me about Burt Mossman."

"Yes."

"You're making a mistake," he said.

"You're not the only man who's told me that," she said.

"But you don't care?"

"No. I don't care."

He watched her with his lips pursed; he said, "Irresistible force, immovable object."

"Not quite." She smiled a little. "I didn't come here to discuss the hopelessness of anything, Judge."

"How do you expect me to be able to explain something if you can't find the answer yourself?"

"I don't expect anything," she said. "I hoped, a little."

He made no answer of any kind. After a while the girl said, "I like the smell of your cigar." Her face moved; she spoke again in exactly the same tone: "Something's breaking him down. Is it that outlaw?"

"You mean Chacon."

"Yes."

"I thought it might be," he said.

Her face came around. She studied him closely. "But now something else has occurred to you?"

"Perhaps," he said, and let it rest there.

"I see," she said, and stood up. "Well, you haven't been reassuring, Judge. Not at all. But you've given me something new to think about."

"Wait," he said. The girl stood arrested by the chair. The judge looked up at her; he said, "If you thought it would solve his problem, would you give him up?"

"No."

"Why not?"

"If I gave him up, it would be because I was trying to help him—it would be because I was thinking of him."

"Why shouldn't you think of him?"

"It would be wrong to think of him," she said.

"I don't understand."

"No," she said; her head was tilted a little. She was decidedly a beautiful woman, he thought. She said, "I don't expect you could understand, Judge." Her face turned on her long neck; she went to the door and left without saying anything further.

Highly puzzled, Judge Williams sat where he was for the better part of a half hour, trying to make out what Ellen Drury had said. But he was completely unsuccessful; the chores of his duty demanded his attention and he went to work at his desk.

CHAPTER VI

FIRST SNOW

The wind whipped Santee's collar up against his face. He rode across a round summit swept barren and dipped into a canyon. The high walls were covered thickly with little round scrubs of manzanita; these were the Patagonia Mountains and this was where the tip had brought Santee.

Clouds had collected, moving up ponderously from the south, from the Mexican Border some five miles away; little flakes of snow fluttered past his face. West a few miles across the humping mountains was the mining community of Washington Camp, built in the groin of two intersecting canyons, and that was his destination; but he had to lay the foundation first, and so he frowned back into his memory, trying to recollect where Pesquiera's adobe shack was. It lay somewhere in these scrub-forested draws, somewhere right around here.

He was five thousand feet up, and the wind had a wicked edge. He pulled his fur-lined gloves up tighter around his wrists and fastened the collar-hook of his coat; he batted his hands against the thighs of his chaps for warmth, and touched his boots to the flanks of his horse, climbing over a ragged hilltop and aiming for the highest single point of land in the vicinity, to get his bearings.

He searched all the pockets of land visible from here, trying to find Pesquiera's shack, and frowned. He swept those angles of the shadowed land with a thorough glance, but learned nothing, and lifted his horse to a canter, heading for another high point of ground from which he could command the whole district. Nothing disturbed the quiet in the cross-canyons below. He had missed something; he frowned again. He backtracked across a dipping saddle and then caught the scent of it, and finally the sight: wood smoke, chimney smoke, drifting up with the wind a quarter-mile away.

He went down the side of the mountain, up the next and down again, and up a third. From this elevation of the trail he swept the hills, spotted the smoke again and turned left toward it, considering the darker, higher reaches ahead. A long distant structure sat down the trail, a long adobe shack set back from the path at the base of the narrow canyon. The wind drummed a constant tone against his chilled ears. He began the descent, dropping into a gully trough and then following a winding, falling trail through the breaks. The high walls about him brought the world close in to touch him, and then dropped away, letting him see the entire panorama of the marching mountains above. In this way, alternately dropping and cutting over hilltops, he pressed into the broken country by a roundabout route until at last he came upon Pesquiera's shack in the canyon.

Four or five dogs started a row when he approached, enough to wake the whole district. They were little dogs, some of them half-coyote, some of them spotted black-and-white and some of them sullen brown in color; they yapped and worried his horse's heels. He sat his saddle in front of the shack and let his call sing out.

A fat woman came to the door, round-faced and brown, and shapeless in a tattered cotton dress. The woman's jet-black hair was thin and dusty, hanging over her head in aimless wisps which she was too indolent to sweep out of the way. She stood heavy in the doorframe, round-shouldered and squinting. Her voice was unfriendly and suspicious. "*Que está?* What is it you want?"

Santee touched his hatbrim. "*Señora Pesquiera—buenos días.*"

A pair of small brown children came around the side of the building, had a look at Santee and disappeared hurriedly, in fright. The woman's lips turned down at the corners. "My husband is not at home."

"*No le quiero,*" Santee said. "I don't want him." His displeased look traveled over the slovenly place and the thin-lipped woman. He said: "A vaquero came through here a few days ago. *Anglo.* He was tall—*mucho hombre.* Riding a roan gelding with an XIT brand. He carries two pistols. Did he stop by here? *Paso por aquí?*"

"*El ley*—the law, it is angry with him?"

Santee shrugged. "Maybe so. Was he here?"

The woman spat. *"No. No estaba."*

"All right," Santee said. *"Gracias y buenos tardes, Señora."* He whirled his pony back to the road, and let it carry him higher along the grades until he was out of sight. Then he looped back to a hilltop overlooking the shack from some distance, and sat watching while the fat woman idled across the yard to the barn. A squat man came out of the barn and the woman spoke quickly, making gestures with her arms. The squat man disappeared into the barn; presently he reappeared leading a saddled horse, and mounted up, nodding perfunctorily to the woman and leaving the yard at a gallop, heading up the road toward Washington Camp.

Santee nodded with satisfaction. It wouldn't be long before that rider down below would take the news to Washington Camp that a Ranger was out batting around in the hills looking for a tall two-gun horseman riding an XIT roan. That was the story Santee wanted to plant; it gave him an ostensible reason to be cruising the Patagonia Mountains. The crew of toughs at Washington Camp probably knew already that Santee was in these hills, and news would go fast enough with that departing rider down below, news of Santee's declared mission. The fact that such a fugitive as he had described to Mrs. Pesquiera did not exist didn't trouble Santee at all.

It was Santee's job today to track down a rumor he had heard, that Augustin Chacon was in the Washington Camp district. Mossman had sent him riding out of Bisbee on many such a mission; this one was probably to turn out as fruitless as all the rest had been. But Santee had his orders.

In the higher mountain reaches the day was dull and cold. His horse climbed into a rocky pass. High-walled red ridges to either side closed down on him until he threaded the floor of the deep gorge, climbed steeply to its head, and soon went by an abandoned outpost gold mine. He topped the ridge beyond and suddenly reined in. Some distance ahead a disturbance in the scrub oak materialized into a rider, moving along before him at a casual but steady gait, and even from afar something about that rider made Santee pause and watch carefully. The rider was tall and very wide across the shoulders, sitting his saddle with military precision. Some vague recollection troubled Santee. And since yonder rider seemed headed in the general direction of Washington Camp, Santee decided to follow him.

The trail lifted him a bit farther, then dropped him around sharp-cut switchbacks so that he lost sight of the horseman for some period of time. When he achieved the top of the next hump he found no sign of the horseman, though his eyes swept the whole vista alertly. He put his horse down the slope, watching the cover to either side with caution. The horseman might have ducked into concealment to watch his back trail. Santee touched his gun. There was a rippling creek ahead; he pulled up within the trees to search both banks before putting his horse across. Ten yards upstream the soft bank was caved in, sign of someone's recent passage, and it was hard to tell whether that track had been left by the rider who had left Mrs. Pesquiera's shack, or by the horseman Santee had seen from the mountaintop. It encouraged him to look for tracks on the other side. But the trail leading up from the creek bank was a heavily trafficked one, packed hard by many travelers, and showed him nothing, so he went up the other side of the depression at a trot, watching warily.

As he approached the climax of this stretch a heavier snow began, chilling with the needle pricks of its flakes. He pulled his hat lower and broke into a canter. Atop the rim of the gulch he saw motion below among the gray trees several hundred yards away from the main trail. He stopped and stood up in the stirrups to watch.

Presently a rider became distinct at the edge of the trees, looked around, and ran across the clearing quickly to disappear into the farther timber.

That one glimpse opened Santee's eyes wider and clenched his gloved fist around the handle of his gun. *Chacon,* he thought, and spoke aloud: "Chacon!"

He put his horse downslope and aimed at the position where he judged Chacon—if it really was Chacon— would reappear from the trees. It was a good half-mile. By the time he reached the spot, Chacon had ridden ahead of him, into the trees across the canyon. Santee followed across quickly, watching the tracks in the soggy soil. He felt the strike of the wind. Circling brought him back on the tracks, chafing at the loss of time, and watching his surroundings closely he lifted to a trot once more. There was no sight of the rider ahead but the broken and indented pine-needle carpet was a book for his eyes to read. He loped along the fresh trail while snow drifted lightly through the branches overhead, and in a short while the tracks dropped him into a road, and disappeared into the traffic there.

He swore a scarlet oath. Chacon might have turned either way along this road; there was no way to tell. From the fork half a mile distant the road led to Nogales, on the Border; to Harshaw and the Black Eagle Mine to the north; and south to Washington Camp. Which way?

FIRST SNOW

His original intent had been to advance to Washington Camp; he decided to gamble and follow that intent. He turned south, passing an abandoned Wells, Fargo depot, and presently came to a small bunch of fresh tracks alongside the road where someone had stopped, possibly to watch the back trail: the horse had fidgeted around and milled, and had then gone on, probably not more than ten minutes ahead, but pushing on at a gallop from the spread of the tracks. It might be a ruse. Santee's squinted eyes studied the surrounding summits thoughtfully. He decided to detour by way of the back country, instead of going straight on down the road: the fugitive might just be waiting for him in ambush on the road.

Therefore he put his horse off the road once more and aimed for the higher ground. Snow came down riding the air currents; he looked at the sky and knew that any moment now the snowstorm would smash down out of the height and breadth of those jagged clouds. From here he guessed it to be perhaps eight, perhaps ten miles to Washington Camp. It was, just now, shortly after noon; it might take him the rest of the day to finish his journey, in bad weather. He bound his hat around his ears like a bonnet with his bandanna; he bowed his head into the wind and let the horse decide on the path, only keeping it pointed south into the wind.

The previous day's warm thaw had hardened by night into a tough crust that remained on the ground today and made bad footing for the horse. His progress was slow; he began hoping he would make Washington Camp by sundown. A strange sensation rolled through him, ruffling his flesh, making him pause and look around. He noticed then that the snow had quit falling, the day was quite still, the crunching of the horse's hoofs was a much louder sound than it should have been. The sky all the while was growing darker. Somewhere in the course of the next hour he felt again that strange premonitory feeling without apparent origin. His stomach was knotted; he blinked against the sky. His face and ears and feet registered the increasing bite of the chill. The temperature was dropping quickly, he knew. He rode through the outbuildings of another abandoned mine and dropped five hundred feet into the trough of a long canyon. The wind rushed forward, all wild crying; day was draining out of the sky even though it was not later than two o'clock, and when he looked at the clouds ahead of him he could see the outline of the tremendous storm marching forward, a spreading abyss pounding ahead in dark fury. The wind's reverberation was a trembling echo; the carpet unrolled quickly overhead, and he broke out of the mouth of the canyon onto an uptilted plain. The touch of a cold finger of wind disturbed the horse and put it into a frightened trot. He kept an uneasy watch on the tall lances of cloud shooting ahead of the boiling storm; he knew he was not going to reach Washington Camp before the storm enclosed him, and he felt a certain fear, knowing he might easily lose himself in the strange night of the storm.

He pushed the horse almost to its limit, cantering up hills where he should have walked the horse, galloping down canyons where he should have trotted; he covered five rugged up-and-down miles in the next hour and stopped on top of a round hill to seek out landmarks.

From here he judged the Camp to be not more than three miles south-by-southwest. He dropped off the crest with the churning force of the storm rushing upon him, a fury of tortured shouts. The pressure of it seized him. It shook him on the saddle, it was a great voice yelling in his ears. In the distance of one mile of travel it became sheets of driving snow and hail.

He could not see the hilltops; he could hardly see the ground at his horse's feet. The storm's great fists battered him; the thrust of the wind made him angle the horse sharply into it to stay on his chosen path. He found a narrow horse trail that he knew led through gullies to Washington Camp, and he set out on that. He fought against the storm with all his energy; he scraped forming frost from his cheeks, saw the moisture of his breath steaming swiftly away, and realized that he could no longer see the earth. All was white.

His legs began to grow numb. He kicked them out in the stirrups, feeling an almost pleasant tingling run up them, and he resolved to defeat the storm—to beat the storm into Washington Camp.

The Camp could not be more than a mile ahead now. He roweled the horse; he felt the horse breaking down under him but he held its head up with the reins and fought against the horse and against the storm, against the world. The wind pressed downward. To the sides he could vaguely see shadowy trees bent by the fury of the weather. He huddled inside his coat, thrusting his feet out and in. He knew if he stopped now, the storm would win. It was a death contest. He rubbed his mittens together and kicked the horse. After a while the path turned dead south, into the wind's teeth, and the horse quit. The horse stood motionless, stiffly braced against the wind, and refused to move on.

As alone as he had ever been, Santee took the reins

and climbed down and went out ahead of the horse. He put his foot down before him and felt it land on nothing.

The most terrifying of sensations slid over him. It was as if the storm in taking away all visibility had somehow removed the earth from under his feet. His foot plunged downward and he swung over the edge of a cliff he had not seen or felt. His hand snapped tight around the reins; he held that instinctive grip and clawed up out of nothingness with nothing more than the horse's head holding him up. He stood trembling; the wind was silence and all sound. He had to fight; he had to go on. "Let's go!" He couldn't hear his own voice, not even in his throat. He felt around for the path, which must have turned; he found it and pulled forward on the reins, leading the horse stubbornly.

In ten minutes he knew this wouldn't do. He was stumbling on unfeeling legs, quickly numbing all over. His nose was stiff and his cheeks raw. He fought; he moved forward.

He jerked himself erect and thought, *Fell into a God-damned snowbank*. He cursed and yanked the horse along and went on, troubled by the necessity of keeping awake and by the inability to do so. He batted his gloved fists against the storm, and felt the weight of his arms. *Ought to lie down—sleepy*. He yanked the reins and pummeled the wind.

A glimmer showed through the snow.

The swirling mist obliterated it after one glimpse but that was enough for him to change course and make for it. Lamplight meant shelter. He waved his arms.

When he saw no light for several minutes, panic touched him. *Maybe I got off*. He turned right, closer into the wind again. *Going in circles—where's that light? Does a blind man feel like this? Damn it, wake up!*

He saw the light again, flickering, to his left. It was brighter, it stayed before him as he approached, and suddenly disappeared as if blown out or covered. *It didn't go out. There must be something between us.*

He walked straight into a wall and bruised his face before he knew of the building's presence. He groped along the wall and found the handle of a big door and pulled it open and plunged inside. The odor of musty ages came out, cold, lifeless, without cheer. The storm reached in past him through the open door, wheeling. This was a barn, the one behind Maldonado's saloon, he thought. He had circled the saloon in the storm and come up behind Washington Camp. He pulled the horse inside the barn. "This will do for you."

He pulled the door shut and spent a few minutes breathing the still air in the barn. His legs were still numb and he walked around, banging into a stall partition and banging into his horse; he jumped up and down, trying to thaw his legs, and presently went outside again, letting the wind slam the door. The wind had enough force to knock him flat against the wall. He felt his way along to the corner and walked on two wooden stalks toward the light, which flickered quite dimly though it was no more than fifteen feet ahead of him. He hit the wall; he searched out the door and banged on it and found the hasp, and wheeled inside.

Someone plunged past him, shouldering the door shut. "Keep that storm out, you fool!"

The storm had got enough of a finger inside to flick out the lamps, plunging the room into profound darkness.

Santee stood dully, in total blackness; it was midafter-noon. Someone struck a match—it was a loud red explo-sion—and then a lamp's oil-wick flame lifted its yellow glow, pushing the shadows back.

The man with the match—Maldonado—went around the dingy saloon lighting lamps. Two or three other men sat around the room, glaring blankly at Santee. Santee felt the close stove heat of the room in his nostrils. He put his gloves, one by one, between his teeth and pulled them off. He tried to unbuckle the fasteners of his coat but his fingers were too numb. When Maldonado, squat and dark, came close to him with his lighted match and lit a wall lamp, Santee said, "Give me a hand, will you?"

Maldonado came close and stood in front of him, un-buckling the fasteners. Maldonado's breath was heavy with whiskey. He said testily, "Anybody tries to buck a storm like this deserves to be dead, cowboy."

"I'm dead," Santee answered. He let his coat slide down off his arms and dropped it on the seat of a chair. He walked forward past the length of the bar and stood near the round black stove, not too close to it, hopping from foot to foot, rubbing his hands up and down his arms and chest, hearing Maldonado's voice, "You need something to drink."

"Yes," he said.

Maldonado came around with a glass of whiskey. "Can you hold this in your hand?"

"Yes. Thanks." He took the glass between his numb fingers, in both hands, and tilted his head back to wash his throat with the warm amber whiskey. Maldonado said, "Feel anything in your legs?"

"A little."

"That's good. Better take off your boots."

"I'll need help."

"All right," the saloonkeeper said.

Santee sat down on a chair and leaned back, holding the chair seat with his hands while Maldonado crouched over his feet and pulled his boots off. Then Santee stood up and went to the stove, standing by it, turning slowly around like a side of beef on a spit. He finished the glass of whiskey and put it on a table. Maldonado took the glass away and brought it back, refilled; Santee said, "Thanks."

"De nada. The Lord watches out for fools."

"Sure." Santee turned his back to the stove for a while. He looked at the three men hunkered around a table across the room. None of them was Chacon, but two owned familiar faces: Billie Stiles and Burt Alvord. The "Humorous Train-Robbers." He knew them from distant and wilder days. He knew they were wanted, and undoubtedly they knew he knew it, but they only sat watching him. The third man at the table got up and went to the bar, and stood there leaning idly, watching no one in particular. Stiles and Alvord looked at Santee without blinking, without expression. Santee said, "Howdy, boys."

"Howdy," Billie Stiles said. He was a little man with round shoulders and beady eyes and a wisp of a mustache over his underslung chin. His partner, Burt Alvord, was tall and broad by contrast, with a glistening dome of a bald head and a flowing cavalry mustache. Alvord's eyes were speculative and amused. He said: "Hello, Santee. Ranger now, ain't you?"

"Yes."

"That's fine," Alvord said quietly. He laid his glance

on Santee like the blade of a razor, motionless but prepared to slice. "Maybe," Alvord said, "you'd better let loose of your gun, Santee."

He couldn't fight the drop. He reached to his thigh, undid the tiedown of his holster, unbuckled the belt and let it drop. Then he stepped back past the stove until his shoulder touched the wall. When he looked at Alvord the cold came in from outside. Alvord stood up indolently, very tall, and crossed the room to pick up Santee's gun; he took it back to the table and laid it there, and sat down again beside Billie Stiles. He said, "Lookin' for us, Santee?"

"I wasn't."

"All right."

"That's enough," Maldonado said from behind his bar. "Ranger, there's coffee on the back of the stove. Help yourself."

"Obliged," Santee said, watching Burt Alvord carefully. Alvord said nothing, did nothing. Santee went back to the stove.

After two cups of coffee, scalding and burning down, his body and mind began to thaw. He faced Maldonado but most of his attention was on the two outlaws at the table. Burt Alvord, the big one, had once been a lawman, the deputy at Tombstone; then he had robbed a train. Stiles had been one of his partners, and had later broken Alvord out of jail. Ever since, the two men had been on the run. Santee watched them without giving away anything in his expression. Life had become like this for Santee, running thin and taut through periods that set his nerves and muscles like triggers waiting to be released. He thought of Cap Mossman and he thought bitterly, *It's not worth it, damn it*. He stared at Alvord and Stiles with his eyes half-lidded. The stove's heat was soporific. Maldonado looked at Santee blankly; Maldonado's glance settled on Burt Alvord for a moment, and slid off. Santee spoke to Maldonado:

"A tall gent on a roan gelding, branded XIT. Seen him in the past two days?"

"You get paid to ask questions," was Maldonado's answer. "It don't pay me to answer them. I'm neutral. I own this saloon—I don't ask nobody for references."

"Sure," Santee said. For some length of time no one spoke. Outside, the storm reached its peak and, by the sound of it, was diminishing in fury. Billie Stiles said, "Where's the outhouse?"

"Through the back door. Ten feet out," Maldonado said.

The flames of the various lamps reflected back from windows turned black by the storm. Shadows flickered across the room and Billie Stiles shook his little shoulders and unbuckled his gun belt casually. He let it drop to the floor and got into a sheepskin coat. "Got to obey the call," he murmured, and fought the back door open, near Santee. The cold rushed inside. Stiles paused for the briefest instant to let a meaningful glance travel across to Burt Alvord; and slammed out.

Squatted by the wall, feeling Burt Alvord's uncertain charged hostility swirling around him, Santee saw the gun encased in Billie Stiles's holster at one corner of his vision, lying on the floor two arm-lengths away.

He sat still. He let the time drag by without stirring until Billie Stiles came back inside to stand with water dripping down from his coat to the gun on the floor. Stiles knelt slowly and picked up the gun. "You didn't have the guts to try it, hey?"

"I guess not," Santee said. "I ain't a fool."

"Smart," Stiles said. "You'll live awhile." He took his gun and went back to the table. Burt Alvord looked at Santee and said: "When the weather lets up, we'll be pushin' on. I expect we'll take your horse with us down the road a mile or so. Then we'll let him loose. Don't follow us—it wouldn't do you any good."

Sure, Santee thought. *But where's Chacon? Where'd he hole up? He's got to be around here somewhere.* What he said was, "Sooner or later your time will come, gents." He took his coffee to a table near the back door and looked around the room. There was a stairway along the back wall going up to an attic room; that door at the top opened now and a Mexican girl appeared at the head of the stairs and came down, showing a flash of ankle and leg, crossing the room to the bar and smiling in a calculated way at Alvord and Stiles, at Santee and Maldonado, and at the other man, the cowboy who had been sitting with Stiles and Alvord and was now at the bar. The girl lifted the cowboy's drink out of his hand in a familiar way, took a sip of the drink and gave it back. The man looked at her and said something softly; the man nodded after he spoke and the girl smiled. Then both of them went across the room past Alvord and Stiles to a door in that side wall. It led into another room, probably Maldonado's kitchen; Santee wasn't sure. The cowboy and the girl went through that door. Santee said, "Got someplace I can bed down, Maldonado?"

"Upstairs," Maldonado said.

"That's not the girl's room?"

"No."

Santee wondered, then, what the girl had been doing

up there. But presently he forgot it. He looked at Burt Alvord and had the distinct impression of looking down the bores of a double shotgun. Alvord looked away, grinning at Stiles. Santee finished his coffee and tilted his chair back against the wall, folding his hands across his thin stomach. That was when the door at the top of the stairs opened again, and Santee's chair came crashing down on all fours. He sat looking upward in wonder and anger.

Standing at the head of the stairway was the tall, gaunt shape of Augustin Chacon. Chacon's handsome face broke into a glistening smile; he rubbed his hands down his thighs and walked slowly down the stairs, still smiling at Santee; he made a point of smiling, and made an equal point of turning away and ignoring Santee thereafter. He went to the table where Stiles and Alvord sat, and Santee noticed the stares of evident dislike mixed with respect and fear that the two outlaws bestowed on Chacon. Outside the wind was dying; it was probably about six o'clock. Chacon spoke briefly to Stiles and Alvord. Chacon's back was to Santee in an insolent way, and Chacon's voice was too low to carry to Santee's ears.

Then Chacon wheeled and faced Santee, still smiling. "I could have stopped you anywhere back there along the trail, *chico*."

Santee regarded him unblinkingly. "Why didn't you?"

"I like to play the game," Chacon said. The manner of his smile told Santee that Chacon was laughing at him. Chacon said, "You will tell your *Capitan* that you caught Chacon here, at Maldonado's."

"I'll tell him."

Chacon's grin widened. "You will tell him also that you let me ride away from here."

"I'll tell him that, too."

Chacon nodded. His grin seemed a natural, habitual part of his expression. "I am sure your *Capitan* will be very pleased with you."

"Your day's comin'," Santee said hotly; he could no longer contain his anger.

"Simmer down," Burt Alvord murmured.

Santee switched his angry glance to Alvord. "What's your piece of this?"

"I'm just mindin' my own business," Alvord said imperturbably. "But you keep a rein on your tongue, boy, or you're a dead man today."

Chacon was ignoring him; Chacon was making answer to Santee's earlier comment: "Yes, my day is coming. Of course. But you see that does not trouble me."

"It will, one day," Santee said.

"I intend to make your *Capitan* pay dearly for me," Chacon said.

Santee glared at him. "Why? Mossman's done nothing to you except what you've deserved."

"He set himself up to run me down. No man has ever run me down." Chacon grinned again. "Did you know I spent two years in the Rurales, under the very nose of the great Colonel Kosterlitzky, and no one ever recognized me? I have defeated greater enemies than your *Capitan* Mossman, my friend."

"No," Santee replied. "You've never run into a man like him before—and you'll find that out."

"Your loyalty is amusing," Chacon said, and chuckled

as if to convince himself. But Santee saw no sign of lessening in the swart-skinned outlaw's cocksureness. Chacon said, "It is an interesting game, is it not?"

"What kind of game?" Santee murmured in a very low tone, and then lifted his voice: "What kind of game, Chacon? How many men have you killed? Twenty-five?"

"Twenty-eight," Chacon answered immediately. "You do not like that, my friend?"

"Maybe they didn't want to die!"

"Ah," Chacon said, chuckling still; "but I wanted them to die, *amigo*. I wanted it—and they died. You see? As long as I want it, I shall play the game—and I shall go on winning the game until I tire of it. You may tell your *Capitan* that. He will not find me until I am ready to be found." So saying, Chacon belted his heavy coat around him and went to the door with long-legged strides. His rugged face turned once, swept the room; then he swung the door back and pushed outside into the diminished force of the storm. Santee rose half out of his seat, but then he heard Burt Alvord's quiet "Uh-uh," and he sat back, disgusted. He had the impulse to hurl something at Alvord's big, stupid, implacable face; but there was nothing to throw, there were only the muzzles of Alvord's black eyes aimed at him and the simpering stare of little Billie Stiles. The wind, cutting under the eaves outside, hummed a lonely tune. Out in the kitchen he heard laughter, the girl and the stranger from the bar. Maldonado came forward from the stove with the coffeepot to pour Santee a fresh cup; and Burt Alvord said, "Relax, everybody."

CHAPTER VII

BORDER CROSSING

That winter, lapping over from 1901 to 1902, was a hard and long one; Santee felt he did a good deal more than earn his fifty-five dollars a month. Once he spent two weeks on horseback in the deep-snow country above the Mogollon Rim, laying siege with another Ranger against a tent-camp of cattle rustlers. On another occasion he rode the length of the Territory from Bisbee to the Grand Canyon, wearing out four horses, on the track of a train-robber; the whole chase took place in below-freezing weather, across succeeding chains of mountains. And always Mossman drove his men, always he demanded a little more of them than he had before; always they responded not with complaint but with a stony kind of eagerness, to please the man who did more than just keep pace with them: he drove himself hardest of all. Mossman seemed in the grip of a mission; and often Santee thought, *You can't do it all at once—slow down—you'll kill us all —we've got longer than overnight.*

More and more often when he was in Bisbee on his infrequent stays there, Santee observed that after the day's work was over Mossman would walk up the hill through Tombstone Canyon to the long-galleried house at the top, Ellen Drury's house. Gossip ran through the town like a fire beyond control; yet none of it touched Mossman; he did not seem to take note of it, though it seemed to be screamed in his ears sometimes. Santee made a point of minding his own business; he did not contribute to the loose talk.

It was on a day in April, after the last snow had melted off the streets, when Mossman came down to the O.K. Stable where Santee was currying his horse. Mossman said: "I've had a report that Chacon and five of his toughs are holed up in a ghost town south of Yuma. We'll take the train."

They took the train, four of them—Mossman and Dayton Graham and Santee and another Ranger, a long lean Texan named Leonard. They left the train at dawn in Yuma, concealed themselves through the hours of daylight, and rode south after sundown leading a pack mule. Santee saw the box of dynamite packed on the mule among the supplies, but he said nothing of it, and no one explained it to him. There was a chill glitter in Mossman's eyes; Santee stayed away from him on that ride.

They crossed the Border into Mexico and went south

along the muddy banks of the Colorado River, threading dense thickets and splashing through marshes under a thick rind of moon that rode downstream with them, dappling the surface of the red-mud Colorado. The night was cool and Santee was damp from the river spray. No one spoke; it was a lonely ride. Santee rode with the ease of long habit, slouched in the saddle, his hat tilted back to his throat vaguely humming the strains of a folk ballad he had learned as a boy in Missouri. He remembered his meeting with Augustin Chacon in Washington Camp last fall and he thought of what Chacon had said, and he said to himself: *Chacon won't make it this easy for us. I don't believe it.* The elusive Chacon had become an image to him, an image of Mossman looking forward; he wondered what would become of Mossman if Chacon were ever run down. He thought of the winter just past, and all the battles fought between Mossman and Judge Williams, between Mossman and Senate President Ives, between Mossman and the newspapers, between Mossman and the governor; Mossman had fought all of them to a standstill; he had allowed no one to curtail his authority; he had pressed relentlessly forward in his campaign, hurling his forces into the mountain fastnesses, sending his men against the outlaw camps, and decimating quite effectively the forces of organized outlawry throughout the Territory. But always there remained the laughing figure of handsome Augustin Chacon. *No,* Santee thought. *We won't get him yet. Not this easy way.*

Colonia was a ghost town some twenty miles south of the Border on the Colorado. Here, on the outskirts, Mossman called a halt at dawn, saying: "Bed down here and get some sleep. We won't move till daylight ends."

Dayton Graham said, "Where you going?"

"I'll scout around a little," Mossman said, and left them. Santee watched him go into the dawn, a bantam figure on horseback with his military posture and the confident set of his head on his shoulders; and Santee thought, suddenly, that he was afraid of Burt Mossman.

"Spread your blankets, boys," Dayton Graham said, and set the example by finding a spot of grass. The ground was dewy, the sky violet in the west and crimson in the east. Santee stretched out with his head on the seat of his saddle, and dozed, a gun near his hand.

The sun came up and warmed his flesh; he moved into the shade at ten o'clock and went back to sleep with an ant climbing over the mountain of his hand. Again in the afternoon the sun came around, moving the shade, and once more he changed his post. This time he remained awake, eating a meal and smoking a cigar, watching waterbugs skim the surface of a little eddying pool cutting back from the river. At six-thirty, with dusk darkening the sky rapidly, Mossman returned to the camp, and everyone rose, clustering around in a little bunch to listen. Mossman crouched down on his heels at the edge of the circle, drawing aimless diagrams in the earth with a stick while he talked:

"The tip was right. There are six of them. They're in a log shack at the north end of town. There's only one family left living in town, and I've asked them to keep their dogs locked up tonight. The horses are in a corral behind the shack and the toughs haven't bothered to post a guard—all six are inside. They play cards until about eight, then they put out the lights. We'll go in about nine-thirty. We'll put two sticks of dynamite at each corner of the shack and blow the walls down, and pick them off as they come out."

"Cap," Santee said.

Mossman's dismal glance came around. "What?"

"Ain't that a little rough?"

"I haven't got time for niceties," Mossman said. "You throw the rules away when you play with Chacon, boy."

"This is Mexico," Santee said.

"Kosterlitzky knows. We've crossed the Border before."

"And played hell every time we did," Santee said.

"Santee," Mossman began, and turned to face him squarely. "If you ever question my orders again, consider yourself discharged from the Rangers."

At nine, Mossman ordered, "Saddle up."

Light was poor that night; a mottled cover of clouds had blown up from the south to hide the moon. The four Rangers rode downstream to a point some hundred yards above the outlaw cabin, and dismounted, leaving their horses ground-hitched. Mossman touched Santee's arm: "Gather here."

The others came up; Mossman handed a pack of fused dynamite to each man. "When you hear my match explode, light your fuses. Let's go—quiet, now."

They slipped through thickets drowned in river spray, turning away from the shore and passing a small grove of trees on their way to the cabin. Twenty yards out they stopped to remove their boots; at ten yards they went down on their bellies, crawling. Through the darkness Santee dimly saw the glint of a knife clenched in Dayton Graham's teeth. Light raced fragmentarily off the blade, reflected from the moon, which came out for two minutes and disappeared once more, after which the four men resumed their stalk.

It took Santee almost ten minutes to cross the last fifteen feet of unprotected open. All the while, his eyes lay steady on the cabin door, expecting it to be flung open at any time. He achieved the back corner without incident and used his hands to scoop out a small hole in the earth by the back of the cabin. Presently the hole was six inches deep and he carefully placed the dynamite in it, pulling up the capped fuse and holding a pair of matches in his hand ready to scratch. The moon came out again and he saw the shape of a crouching man at the far back corner —Dayton Graham, waiting with his match. Graham's hat brim rose and fell, a nod of reassurance, and Santee moved enough to look past the side wall to the front corner where Mossman squatted. Another minute went by, during which a cloud passed the moon and a chicken clucked somewhere down in the ghost town below. Then the brilliant flare of Mossman's match burst, and Santee sat fascinated by it for a broken instant before he reacted by lighting his own paired matches and holding them against the fuse. At first it did not catch; the matches burned half down before the fuse began to spit and glow, and Santee was sure a gun would start firing out through the cabin window. But now the fuse was lit and Santee stood up softly, seeing Dayton Graham coming forward in his socks with long steps. Graham came by, touching his shoulder, squeezing it once; he turned and followed Graham's shadow-figure down past the side of the cabin, and met Leonard and Mossman at the front. Thereupon the four of them walked steadily away from the cabin to the small grove of trees where they had left their boots. Santee heard Mossman's dead-calm voice: "Drop flat."

He dropped. His shoulder butted the bole of a tree; he looked past the trunk at the cabin, and thought he saw a faintly sputtering spark at one corner. He felt a slow regret; he started to say, "Cap," but he didn't have time; the dynamite erupted in a great bloom of light and sound.

The house shattered slowly, as if each of its logs was carried by a different slow current of water. The corners, rocked away from their bases, fell down and then the walls fell away slowly, and in the quick afterglow of the explosion Santee saw the roof lift, all in one piece, and slowly tilt, sliding away over the back wall. There must have been four separate explosions, but he only heard the one, and saw the extending blast of white light. Afterward there was a dead blackness for an instant; the explosion had blinded him. His ears rang with a sibilant whistle. A fire had begun among the twisted logs and by its quickly growing light he saw a number of men scrambling around in confusion; he heard Mossman's very quiet order, "Pick them off."

Someone fired a shot, then another, and Santee felt his hand clutching at his rifle; he brought it to his cheek and sighted along the barrel, and brought one staggering figure up to the top of his bead sight; his thumb eared back the rifle hammer and he squeezed the trigger evenly, holding his breath. The rifle recoiled against his shoulder. The shot was very loud; he saw the tongue of flame lick from his own rifle barrel and he saw the man who was his target pitch forward and lie broken across a heap of smoldering logs. Around Santee, the rifles had opened up in earnest, and there were three quick volleys of fire, almost in unison. Then the shooting became sporadic, as each man picked out a target. Once, dimly, Santee thought he saw a running figure going away behind the cabin, but he wasn't sure. He jacked a fresh cartridge into the rifle chamber and fired, missing his target, and loaded again. When he took aim there was no target. There was only the collapsed heap of rubble and the strewn bodies of men. He heard someone say, "That's all." And he let down the hammer of his rifle to safety-cock.

Mossman spoke calmly: "Get your boots on. I think one man got away."

Santee used up a little time finding his boots where he had left them. Then he tugged them on and followed Mossman to the cabin site. A few small fires were burning among the logs, enough to see by. Five bodies lay around what had been the front of the cabin. Mossman went among them, touching them with his toes, turning two over to see their faces. All of them were dead; none was Chacon.

"Come on," Mossman said, and not understanding him, Santee followed, hurrying to catch up. Mossman was dog-trotting back toward the river, toward where they had left their horses. Presently Santee passed through the river thickets and almost blundered into Mossman's back. Mossman was standing near the riverbank, looking at the three horses there, and Mossman was chuckling. Santee looked at him with amazement. "What's funny?"

"Chacon," Mossman said. "He picked a particular horse. My horse."

"Hell," Santee said, "are you trackin' down a killer, or picking an opponent for a card game?"

Mossman didn't answer; he only pointed to Santee's horse and said, "Go on back and get the pack mule. Bring those shovels up here."

CHAPTER VIII

NO COMPROMISES

"I just can't bring myself to understand it," Judge Williams said.

"The only thing I can't understand," Mossman replied, "is how four of the best rifle shots in the Territory could have missed him. He was set up for us, a silhouette target —and he made it away clean, again."

"I don't care a whit about Chacon," the judge said angrily. "You slaughtered five men down in Mexico without a damn bit of excuse. You could have called on them to surrender."

"Not Chacon," Mossman said quietly.

"How do you know? Have you ever tried?"

Mossman only gave him a very slight smile. The judge leaned forward, planting his elbows on his desk. "There's absolutely no justification for what you did down there. It was outright murder."

"Has Kosterlitzky complained?"

"No."

"Has any Mexican official complained?"

"No."

"Then you have no grounds to censure me," Mossman said.

"Good God, man—it's a question of human morality!"

Mossman shook his head. He was standing by the window, looking out over the Bisbee Plaza, and now he turned to face the judge grimly. He said: "The Rangers aren't a police force, Judge, and we can't be expected to act like a police force. We're an army. We are engaged in a war against what I consider an armed invasion. We're fighting a campaign against organized toughs, and we're outnumbered terribly. I make use of the most effective methods available to me. That's all I can tell you by way of an answer; I don't make excuses and I don't make apologies, for my men or for myself."

"I won't accept it," the judge said flatly. "It's not good enough, Burt. Five dead men— My God, five!"

"A skirmish," Mossman murmured. "A tactical maneuver. Do you quibble about minor tactical arguments in the midst of a strategic battle, Starr?"

"I'm talking about lives," Judge Williams said, not budging from his issue. "I'm talking about five men who should have had the chance at a trial. Is that minor? Is that a tactical argument, Burt? It wasn't, to those five men who died."

"Lives," Mossman said, in an utterly bland tone. He came forward to lean against the judge's desk, facing him, his arms straight against the desk edge. "Starr, for those five gunnies it was all written down in the book long before they crossed the Border with Chacon. They wrote their tickets when they picked Chacon for a traveling companion."

"You sound like an Old Testament patriarch," Judge Williams grumbled. "You haven't changed the facts, Burt, and you won't. Five men were butchered down there, without benefit of a hearing."

"They had their hearing," Mossman said softly. "They made their choice."

"Some of them might have had families."

"I don't care. I don't care who they were. It makes no difference."

"They were *men*, Burt. Men with God-given souls."

"They sold their souls."

"To the devil?"

"To Augustin Chacon," Mossman said.

The judge shook his head. "No. It won't wash. I can't condone it."

"I don't ask you to condone it."

The judge gave him an exasperated glance. "Burt, you don't get this yet. I've pushed and pleaded and pried the boys up in Phoenix. I've done everything in my power to keep them off your back. But I can't keep it up if you continue to slap law and order in the face. You'll lose your job—the whole Ranger movement will be abandoned—and the Territory will be right where it was a year ago. Do you want to see the Rangers disbanded?"

"I'd rather see them disbanded than see them kowtow to the whims of politicians."

"Hell," the judge snorted. "You're an idealist."

"Of course I'm an idealist."

"But you're a murderer. How do you reconcile that?"

"I don't consider myself a murderer. I don't think I've taken anything that wasn't mine to take. It was in the nature of my job to kill those men, Starr."

"Then you misunderstand your job," Judge Williams said flatly. "The law does not condone murder."

"I've committed executions," Mossman said. "Not murders."

"No."

Mossman regarded him with his customary bleak gaze, impenetrable and level. Then he swung with a snap of his shoulders and returned to the window, setting his short frame up there, looking out on the town. Judge Williams kept his eyes on Mossman's profile. When Mossman looked at him, he saw impersonal gravity in Mossman's expression. Mossman lit a stubby cigar and held it between his short, firm fingers; and when he spoke he spoke carefully, choosing his words deliberately. "Where are your people from, Starr?"

"Sir?"

"Your family. They must have come from some part of Europe at some time."

"Yes," the judge said. "Of course."

"Why did they come?"

"I don't know," he answered, and frowned. Mossman seemed to be leading him away from the direction he had started, and he felt irritated. "Why should that matter?"

NO COMPROMISES

Mossman slid the window open and tapped his cigar outside. His back was ramrod stiff; the gate before him had not been let down. He said: "A very short while ago, your ancestors and mine were citizens of ancient and well established civilizations. They regulated themselves, so they said, by codes of law and morality that went back thousands of years. Some of those codes were right, some weren't. It took all those years of slow construction to build up civilizations. Then those people came from that background to this country. Within fifty years half of them had become savages and the other half had shut themselves up behind a thin front of gentility in towns, so that they could ignore the ones who had become savages."

Listening to the flat ring of Mossman's words, the judge was surprised by this display of sensitivity. He said, "Go on."

"It took an unusual kind of man," Mossman said, "to push across the frontier. Call him by an old bromide—call him a rugged individualist. But the others, the ones who didn't have enough toughness, fell out. They turned back, or they quit and died, or they came because they smelled a profit but they brought their whole background with them like a shield—big Georgian houses and servants in livery. And then, of course, a good many of them just died."

"What do you mean?"

"I mean this," Mossman said. "It took a thousand years to make a civilized man, and a single generation to turn him back to barbarism. Now, I've taken a job—and my duty according to this job is to bring back the civilization that we've lost. My job is to eliminate the savages. Back

East and in Europe, or wherever there's a closed society with traditions, a great many influences keep most people in line—public opinion, established law, churches and families and loyalties of all kinds. But out here we've got no traditions. Men grow up isolated. They don't abide by laws because they seldom have contact with laws and they haven't been taught to respect them."

"I thought," the judge interrupted him, "that you despised organized authority."

"I don't despise it," Mossman said. "I recognize it, I know what it is, I live according to my attitudes toward it—not according to my ignorance of it. You see the difference? These toughs have been bred in the wilderness. They don't abide by custom because there isn't any custom. They've got no consideration for society because they didn't grow up in a society. They're not interested in themselves, as individuals—they're not interested in anything. They destroy instinctively. They steal because they haven't got enough pride to work. They sleep under a wagon with their heads on saddles. When they're hungry they shoot animals; when they're cold they build fires. They don't recognize the necessity for self-respect—all they want to do is survive. They know that a man who doesn't fight will die, but the only way they're capable of fighting is a primitive way. Their lives are threatened so much that they don't have any regard for the value of their own lives or their own property. They live to plunder, just as I live to work."

The judge's voice was almost a whisper, "What are you getting at, Burt?"

"When you deal with that kind of man," Mossman said, "you've got to deal with him in a primitive way. He doesn't understand anything else. The only thing he knows how to respect is a man tougher than himself. That's why I'm tough, Starr—my job demands it. The only way to make a tough obey the law is to back the law with a gun, and back the gun with a man who knows how to use it. That's why I've made it my business to make myself a legend, to announce to all the toughs that I'm tougher than any of them. And that's why I can't afford to let Chacon escape me. If he gets away, I've failed—and the toughs won't respect me. I won't fail, Starr. Not if it takes five dead men or fifty. The toughs have got to respect my fighting ability. As long as I have that respect, the law has respect too."

He subsided into silence. Judge Williams murmured, "You have a hard philosophy, Burt."

Mossman did not answer; he seemed unwilling to carry the talk further. It was a source of wonder to the judge that Mossman had spoken as much as he had.

Mossman crossed the room with measured strides to the door. He looked at the judge and said a strange thing: he said, "It's not necessary that you understand, Starr." And left.

My God, the judge thought. He went to the window, standing in Mossman's footsteps, and looked out on the dusty Plaza and the steep canyons above.

CHAPTER IX

HOUSE ON THE MOUNTAINTOP

The heat of the summer night came in through the roof, through the walls, pressing her; she touched her hands to her cheeks and went across the dark room to open a curtain and push the window up, hoping for a draft of air to come through the room; none did. Down below, past the window and the hill, she saw a milling crowd eddying in an aimless whirlpool around the Plaza and the foot of Brewery Gulch and O.K. Street; and up higher, more to her left, she could see the glow of the Brewery Gulch lights like a pale dawn over the undulations of School Hill and the High Road. There was no moon. The stars were a pale wash, with now and then a distinct glittering sparkle where one brighter star showed through the haze of dust in the air.

She went across the dark parlor again, not wanting to light a lamp, and stood by the open front door looking out across the porch, down the path he would come up. It was a rock-bordered walk bounded by the lawn, a walk of dust and vague heelprints. Down the hill a little way one light glowed quite sharply at the back of someone's house. There was a soft ring of dust around the light; she wished someone would put it out. With several unconnected thoughts idling past her mind, she made a purposeless circuit around the room and came back to the front door, and stood there with her arms folded across her breasts, feeling the push of time driving forward, feeling the quiet loneliness of the hilltop. Her mind was clothed in a mist of uncertainty.

She went back to the kitchen, not wanting to know what time it was. The stove glowed through slits around the edges of the burners. The blackened coffeepot bubbled slowly and outside a breath of wind disturbed the leaves crisply. She felt the warmth of the night and of the stove making her mildly sleepy.

She heard a step, and went to the parlor door, and saw his trim form outlined on the porch, coming forward; he stood for a moment with his shoulders cutting a solid block against the doorway, and she spoke across the room to him, "I'm here."

Mossman tarried briefly where he was, then advanced into the room. He did not approach her, but went to the far window and waited motionless. His head was in silhouette against the window; his face was only a dark suggestion. She stood silent with her thoughts and felt a quick irritation at her inability to see his expressions, and presently she moved down the length of the wall to light a lamp.

"Don't," he said.

She paused with her hand lifted, an unlit match in her fingers. "Why?"

His answer was some time coming. He turned so that a little of the starlight struck his features; his face was the color of marble, no warmer. There was no motion in his expression. His lips were set into a long, straight line under the droop of his mustache.

"Why?" she said again, in a tone meant to rouse him.

His pulse throbbed visibly at his neck. "Never mind," he said. "Go ahead. Light the lamp."

"Not if you'd rather I didn't."

His lips pinched in. It was the only sign she had of his feelings. "It makes no difference," he said. "Light the lamp."

She shook her head and went to a chair, and sat, made reflective by what had just occurred. "Are you afraid of the light?"

He didn't reply. Then, somewhere in the course of the ensuing moments, she heard his grunt and saw him push away from his post. He came forward past her and struck a sudden match and lit the lamp. Then he stood by it in an apparent state of indecision. Ellen blinked against the brightness. She felt an awkwardness had come into the room; Mossman had regained his distance and now held it coolly.

"It's a nice night. I like the dark," she said, and waited his further comment.

There was none. When Mossman took a chair, she noticed he moved it aside from the window before he sat down. She thought she understood, then; he did not want to be framed in the window from without. Beyond the sill, blackness eddied in wide sweeps over the land's deeper pockets, with now and then the pale summit of a hill showing. A buggy, heard but not seen, came up along the Tombstone Canyon road at a rapid clip and faded into the distance. Ellen said, "If I knew why you didn't want me to light the lamp, I might have an answer to some of my questions. Was it just to keep from being a target?"

"No," he said.

"What, then?"

"A moment of weakness," he said. "It's not important."

"Perhaps it is."

"You've no cause to be that concerned."

In his gentle tone rode the definite suggestion that he would prefer to see the subject dropped. But it was, so far, one of the very few loopholes she had found in him, in his defense; and the very fact that he had a defense made her want to overcome it. She pressed: "Are you forbidding me to ask the question?"

"I've never forbidden you anything."

"Then I'll make a guess," she said. "You had me at an advantage before that lamp was lit. You could see my face, but I couldn't see yours—and you didn't have to maintain your own expression."

He said nothing; she prodded him, "I don't know why you should want to hide you feelings from me."

His shoulders rose, almost imperceptibly, and dropped. "Call it habit."

"No," she answered, "I don't believe I will."

"As you will," he said. She shook her head; his defense

was still closed up and she felt defeated. She knew he would not let her push him much further; yet she said, "I worry about you, Mossman."

"That's unwise."

She smiled a little. "Can't you even relax? Must you be so formal with me?"

"Am I formal with you?"

"Yes."

He smiled a little; he lit a cigar and turned in his arm-chair, so that his leg hung over one arm and he was coiled sideways in the chair. He watched her with meaningful blankness in his expression and she laughed at him; her head went back and she laughed quite strongly. And heard Mossman speak drily: "That's better, now."

She remembered the coffeepot in the kitchen, and still chuckling, she went out of the room. When she returned she handed him his cup and returned immediately to her own seat, and said, "Last time you came you spoke of that Ranger of yours—Santee."

"What of it?"

"You didn't finish."

"What was I saying?"

She laughed again. "I don't really remember. But it stuck in my mind; I remember thinking that it seemed strange that you would show any interest in him. In him or in anyone."

"I'm not as cold-blooded as all that," Mossman murmured. "Santee interests me because he's not particularly intelligent and doesn't have any particular abilities, and yet he's been able to make his own decisions without being pushed around. When I see a man like Santee, it makes me think there's hope for all of us. Santee's not conceited, but he's sure enough of himself to make his own decisions—he doesn't let anyone make up his mind for him. When he quit that outlaw crew it was strictly on his own initiative."

Mossman tapped his cigar ashes outside; he was not looking at Ellen, but aimlessly at the floor. He said, "Santee's afraid of me, in a way, but he's not afraid of talking back to me. That's a good sign too."

"Is it? It shows bad discipline."

"The only worthwhile discipline a man can get is the kind that comes from himself," Mossman said. "It's easy to take orders from someone else. Taking orders from yourself—that's hard. Santee obeys my orders, because it's his job to obey them. But he's responsible enough to question my orders. If he didn't have that much pride, I wouldn't have him."

"Mossman," she said, and shook her head. "That boy's your soft spot. You're not his father."

"Well," he murmured in easy answer, "I suppose a man's entitled to a soft spot or two." He smiled in a lazy way; he was loosening up. It always took time, but eventually she knew she could make him relax. It was only a matter of relieving the pressure on him. Still, she felt urged to speak:

"You know, I don't really think your young Ranger's much different from most people."

"Maybe he's not," Mossman said. "But he's not as willing to run with the herd as the rest of them are."

"Perhaps that's not good for him."

"It's harder to do. In the long run it's good for him— it's good for any man to learn the value of self-respect. We're not cattle. If we take orders, it's because we choose to take orders—that's the nature of democracy. Santee understands that. That's why I like him."

He sat silently thereafter, smoking his cigar, and after a while Ellen said, "Do you know, that's the first time I've ever heard you say you liked someone?"

"Is it?" His tone was vague. His face displayed no particular expression, nothing out of the ordinary, yet she felt he was relaxing thoroughly. His head came around slowly and he gave her a stare of evident gravity. It disturbed her; her own expression took on a sharper cast. It boosted her up out of the chair, still holding her coffee, the cup in one hand and the saucer in the other. She went around the room, bobbing from point to point, and came to a restive halt near the kitchen door, where she turned and regarded him flatly. Her eyelids were close; anger stiffened her. She said, "You're a thousand miles away, Mossman —you always have been."

"I'm sorry. I can't help that."

"I know," she said quietly; she turned out of the room to put her cup in the kitchen, and came back to face him with bleak sadness. "What would it mean to you if I said I was in love with you?"

"You'd be making a mistake," he said evenly. He met her glance; she found nothing in his eyes.

She said: "A mistake—I guess so. But I've said it now. Dayton Graham told me a long time ago I was a fool."

"He's a wise man."

"Oh, hell," she said loudly, and went back to her chair. She experienced a turmoil of thoughts; she said to him: "You could rebuff me, at least. You could make me feel as though I've said something."

"Is that what you want me to do?"

"I don't know," she said. "The one thing I really want you to do is the one thing you can't do."

"I'm sorry."

"No," she said. "That's just words."

"If that were true, I wouldn't have said it."

Angry with him and angry with herself, she lifted her head and looked directly at him. She said, "I intend to keep after you, you know."

"I expect you will."

"I intend to break down your damned defense, Mossman."

"You can try."

"I will try. And you'll let me try."

"Why should I?" he said.

"Because you've got to know whether I can do it. If I can break down your defense, then you're all through, Mossman—and you've got to know whether I can do it. You've got to *know*—otherwise you'll never again be so damned positive about yourself." She subsided; she let the room become silent. Then she said: "I've always let my shrewdness and my money make up for people. I've never needed people. But I need you."

He only said again, "I'm sorry."

CHAPTER X

HEMP JUSTICE

It was cloudy in the south. Santee swung off the walk before the English Kitchen, feeling the weight of his breakfast hanging in his stomach, and went slowly across the dusty Square, stopping once and waiting to let a heavy ore wagon pass, drawn by ten teams of mules, with the muleskinner riding the off wheel mule, cracking his whip. The wagon lumbered past and Santee coughed against the dust, continuing on to the post office and up the steps.

In the short hallway he paused; he was about to enter Mossman's office but across the hall the door to Judge Williams' office was ajar and Santee heard Mossman's voice, "Mr. Ives, it isn't your affair to meddle in my department."

Santee stepped into the room and moved aside from the door, putting his back to the wall, saying nothing; he only removed his hat and nodded to Judge Williams, who sat behind his desk watching Mossman. Mossman was talking to E. S. Ives, the Territorial Senate President. Santee had met Ives two or three times; Ives dipped his head toward Santee now but did not speak to him. Ives returned his attention to Mossman, saying: "Your company was set up by the Legislature, Burt, and it can be destroyed the same way. Word is spreading that you've put known outlaws on the payroll of the Rangers—and we can't have that."

"I've hired no known outlaws," Mossman said. He stood—or rather, leaned—hipshot against the widowsill, looking completely unconcerned. Santee knew him well enough to know that Mossman was listening to Ives with full attentiveness. Ives said: "You know perfectly well what I mean, Burt. Sometimes the line drawn between a back-country tough and a known outlaw is hard to find."

"On the contrary, Mr. Ives, it's quite plainly marked. Santee?"

"Yes, sir."

"Would you have classified yourself as a back-country tough before I hired you?"

"I don't know," Santee said. "Maybe."

Mossman nodded and turned back to Ives. "Santee is one of the best men I've got."

Ives glanced at Santee, and back at Mossman. "Are you willing to stake the character reputations of your Rangers against the results of a legislative investigation of your organization?"

"I'm willing to stake the results I achieve on the abilities of my men," Mossman replied evenly.

"That's not the same thing at all."

"How far do you think I'd get if I hired a pack of quiet citizens with impeccable records, Mr. Ives?"

"Do you admit by that you've hired questionable people?"

"No," Mossman said. "I don't question them at all." Santee was beginning to know him well enough to suspect that the slight disturbance of his lip corners represented a smile. Mossman went on: "Court records are open to investigation, Mr. Ives. So are my financial books. Beyond that, the Rangers' activities are not a matter of record. I would advise against an investigation on your part—you wouldn't find much evidence in support of either side."

"Damn it," Ives muttered, "I wish you wouldn't call me Mr. Ives. We're friends, Burt."

Mossman didn't answer directly; what he said was: "You disapprove of my methods. I think it's safe to say I find it best to fight fire with fire."

"Toughs with toughs, you mean. But a man can also fight fire with water, Burt. If I were in your boots I'd watch my step—I'd take care to think about consequences." Ives was a little ruffled; he was, just now, turning toward the door.

Mossman's face lifted. "Wait."

Ives stood fast. "What is it?"

Mossman regarded him without blinking. "Mr. Ives, you speak of consequences. I see only two possible consequences. Either I'm given free rein, to accomplish the job I've been assigned, or the mealy-mouthed cowards who sit behind their walls will defeat me first, and Arizona will return to savagery."

Ives' shoulders turned; otherwise he didn't move. He looked slantwise at Mossman and after a moment his voice came, thoughtful and slow, "Do you really hate us that much, Burt?"

"I don't hate you—I don't hate anybody."

"Then you're a hell of a conceited man."

"That may be," Mossman acknowledged. "But don't ever make the mistake of assuming a soft man can do a hard man's job. I've been given a job and I'm doing it the best way it can be done. If I fail it won't be because my methods were the wrong ones; it will be because my methods suffered too much interference from people who are plainly not qualified to judge my methods."

"Are you sure of that?" Ives said. "Burt, you've got a weakness—you're not a politician."

"No. I'm a soldier."

"I'm afraid you'll discover it's not enough," Ives said, a little stiffly; he turned and walked out, brushing Santee's shoulder.

"He'll calm down," said Judge Williams.

Mossman nodded. He waggled a finger at Santee and left. Santee followed him across the hall into the Ranger office; he closed the door and said, "Did he mean what he said about a legislative investigation?"

Mossman's shoulders rose and fell. "Maybe—maybe."

"You know, he may be right, Cap. You ain't much of a politician."

"It's not your concern to worry about that," Mossman said. He sat down behind his small desk and opened a drawer.

"Damn it, I just thought maybe I could help."

"You can help by following orders," Mossman said mildly, signing a requisition and folding it into an envelope. "Within the last forty-eight hours I've had four telegrams. One from Yuma, one from Flagstaff, one from Kingman and one from Harshaw. All of them are from peace officers who claim Chacon's been seen in their bailiwicks in the past two days."

"Ain't possible," Santee said promptly. "Nobody's got wings, not even Chacon."

"I know. Chacon's more of a rumor than a man. Every time some Mexican or Indian commits a crime, as long as he fits a basic description they'll blame Chacon every time. It's my feeling that half the criminals in Arizona are riding scot-free because somebody mistakenly identified them as Chacon and pinned the crimes on him. Chacon's our number one problem, boy."

"Maybe," Santee said. He was thinking of Ives, and the politicians. "Maybe."

"I want him," Mossman said gently, and sealed the envelope.

That was when knuckles rapped the door. Santee looked around. "Who's that?"

"Telegram."

Santee opened the door and accepted the telegram, crossed the room and handed it to Mossman. He waited while Mossman read the wire. Mossman grunted, stood up and reached behind him for his coat on the wall hook. "Saddle up."

"Where to?"

"Nogales. Jethro Drew held up the cantina."

"Jethro Drew? He's one of Chacon's men, ain't he?"

"Chacon's lieutenant," Mossman said. He was on his way to the door.

Jethro Drew's trail took them from the railhead at Nogales westward along the desert hills, following the line of the Mexican Border until they reached the point where the Border tilted northwestward. Then the tracks turned due north and Santee said, "Maybe he's headed for Ruby."

"Possibly," Mossman said.

There had been no time to gather more men; there were only the two of them riding on Drew's track, and the trail was getting cold. Drew had ten hours on them.

This part of the Territory was dry country, humping hills covered with scrubs and yucca, and wide creosote flats. The outlaw's trail took them almost as far as Ruby, then doubled back abruptly and aimed southwest toward the Organ Pipe Cactus area. Santee pushed his horse to keep up with Mossman; they did not make camp until almost midnight, and rode forward again at dawn. At ten o'clock they passed the ashes of a campfire and Mossman said, "We've cut his lead in half."

At noon the temperature had climbed well above the hundred-degree mark. Santee squinted narrowly across the shimmering plain. Bridle metal at his horse's jaw sent painful flashes against his eyes; he heard the clop of hoofs and the creak of leather; he felt the warm oil of sweat along his body. A little wind came up, bringing no relief, whipping his cheeks as though it were full of hot sand. The sun beat against his shoulders, pushing them down. He tilted his hat forward and took a sip from his canteen, working the water around in his mouth with his tongue; the water was hot enough to scald. He dismounted once to pick up a pebble and put it in his mouth, and rolled it around his teeth to keep his saliva working. When he looked at Mossman he saw no evidence of discomfort in the man, but only a blank sort of deliberateness. Mossman's eyes lay on the ground ahead, the faintly indented tracks of a single horse extending off into the distance.

They crossed the Border near nightfall and rode straight through the night, traveling slowly under the high moon, seeking out the tracks. Jethro Drew had not bothered to hide his trail. It led them as far as the shore of the Gulf of California at Sierra Prieta, which they reached at about dawn; they spent that day combing the little mud town, finding nothing, and slept through most of the afternoon, after which they circled the back of town, looking for horse tracks leading away. There was only one set of tracks, which was a piece of luck; they followed it southeastward across the hills to the Rio de la Altar, and almost lost the trail there.

Santee combed the banks of the thin stream and presently heard a faint hail. When he looked up through the pale dawn he saw Mossman on a grassy hilltop, waving his arm in signal. Santee splashed across the river and rode up; he looked down at the tracks, nodded, and put his horse on the trail beside Mossman's. It was the third day of their treck; on the morning of the fifth day they achieved the canyon of the Rio Nacozari and saw the rise of smoke past a small bend in the canyon; Mossman halted. "There's a good chance Drew's not alone in that camp."

"Chacon?"

"Maybe," Mossman said. "Or there may be half a dozen toughs. We'll take it easy."

They dismounted short of the bend. Mossman spoke in a low voice, "There may be a guard posted around here." He led the way up the back of the hill; somewhere on the far side of it was that campfire. Santee took care placing his feet; he made no sound, making the slow ascent through trees and grass; and near the top, Mossman motioned to him, indicating that they would split up here, Mossman going to the right and Santee to the left.

Santee used a good deal of caution over the next twenty minutes, topping the hill and creeping forward, threading the stunted trees to a point from which he could command the camp below. Then he spent a silent, motionless quarter hour studying the scene below, after which he moved to a new vantage point and repeated his survey. Down below was a small fire surrounded by the barren openness of a wide clearing. Tethered not far away was a single horse. One man sat crouched near the fire; it was a cool morning in the mountains. That man rose to his feet once, went to his grounded saddle and took something from a saddlebag—probably food. He returned to the fire and hunkered down again. Other than that, and the horse's quiet browsing in the grass, there was no activity in sight. Santee's inspection was long and thorough enough to convince him there was only one man in the meadow below.

"Easy, Santee."

The murmured words whipped his head around; he saw Mossman crouched on his heels not five feet away. Santee swallowed. "You'd have made a hell of a good Indian."

"Probably," Mossman agreed. "See anything?"

"Just that one gent. Jethro Drew?"

"We'll see," Mossman said. "You've never met Drew?"

"No."

"Then I'll have to guess from the wanted poster picture. Let's go down and have a talk with him."

They went down carefully, crossing the intervening space in twenty minutes and coming up silently behind the crouching camper.

"Don't move a whisker," Mossman said in a conversational tone. His revolver was out, trained on the crouching man's back. Santee saw that man's shoulders stiffen but otherwise there was no movement. "All right," Mossman said. "My gun's on you, friend. Stand up and turn around."

The camper stood and turned slowly, keeping his arms spread wide from his body. He was tall and darkly bearded; his eyes were narrow slits. He stood fast, displaying no fear, and Mossman said, "Jethro Drew."

"Sure," said that man.

"I'm Mossman."

Jethro Drew's eyes opened a little wider, and closed down again. "So what?"

"This is an arrest."

"Don't make me laugh. This ain't Arizona—this is Mexico."

"Think of that," Mossman murmured with a cutting dryness. "Unbuckle your shell belt and let it drop. That's good —now step away from it."

Drew obeyed. "You'll never make this stick, fellow."

"My gun says you're wrong." Mossman stood silent a moment, thinking of something, and then said to Santee,

"This is one of Chacon's camps—the grass is grazed down and there are half a dozen dead fires around here. Chacon will be back, sooner or later."

Jethro Drew grinned. "You plan to wait for him? You'll have a long wait, Ranger. He'll smell you out from ten miles away."

"We won't wait," Mossman murmured. "But I intend to leave him a message."

Drew's forehead showed wrinkles; the start of troubled thoughts showed in his eyes. "Wait a minute," he said, and trailed off, watching Mossman with a cornered man's tautness.

Mossman spoke to Santee: "Tie his hands behind him with his belt. Then saddle up his horse."

Santee went forward, taking the precaution of handing his own gun to Mossman before he approached the outlaw. He pulled the belt out of Drew's trousers and lashed the man's hands together behind him. Then he took Drew's saddle across the meadow to the tethered horse and cinched it up. When he turned around he saw Mossman walking down toward the river, prodding Drew ahead of him. Santee frowned, trying to figure out what Mossman was doing; he untied Drew's horse and led it forward, following Mossman.

Mossman stopped on the river bank underneath the spread of a tall cottonwood; when Santee came up, Mossman said, "This will do. Mount up, Drew."

Santee had to help the bound man up into his saddle. When he turned to look, he saw that Mossman was fashioning a knot in the end of a hemp rope. Santee's face moved; he said, "Cap—what the hell?"

"A message for Chacon," Mossman answered, and

tossed the end of the rope over a limb of the cottonwood.

Just getting this now, Drew said, "Hey—wait a minute!" And hopped off his horse, losing his balance and falling on his face.

Santee jumped forward, pinning Drew down; he looked up at Mossman. "You can't do this, Cap."

"Put him on his horse," Mossman said, "and tie his feet under the horse's belly if he doesn't quiet down."

Santee stepped away and Drew staggered to his feet. "God damn you—you can't get away with this, Ranger!"

"You killed two men when you robbed that saloon."

"What of it? That don't give you the right to kill me without a trial."

"He's right, Cap," Santee said.

Mossman only stood fast, his gun hanging in his fist. "Mount him up, Santee."

The light in Mossman's eyes was cold and bleak. Santee thought of the snowstorm he had weathered last winter. "Put him on his horse," Mossman said again. Jethro Drew was watching Mossman with fascinated terror; Drew moved like a mechanism, as though his body were moving against his will. Santee pushed him up into the saddle. Drew sat sweating, his eyes wide and round, staring down at Mossman. There was no particular expression on Mossman's face. The noose hung down from the cottonwood limb; Mossman said, "Put the noose over his head, Santee."

"No. I ain't going to have any part in this, Cap."

"Put the noose over his head."

Santee stood his ground. He shook his head. Mossman said: "I intend to leave him here as a message to Chacon. Grab the noose, Santee—I won't say it again."

"God damn it," Santee said quietly, "you can talk all

morning and I won't hang him, Cap. Listen—if I had my gun I'd stop you."

Mossman looked down; Santee thought he was changing his mind, but then he saw that Mossman was only looking at Santee's gun in his own waistband. When Mossman looked up again he said a strange thing: he said, "You're a good man, Santee."

"I think I am," Santee said viciously. He could stand no more of this; he wheeled and plunged across the meadow, running; he crashed upward through the brush and stopped only when he reached the top of the hill. He turned, looking back—and saw the figure of Jethro Drew dangling from the cottonwood limb. Mossman's shape was small and still. "Jesus," Santee whispered. "No!" He spun off the hill and ran down toward his horse in the farther canyon.

CHAPTER XI

"CAP!"

He rode the hills of Mexico for a week. He saw no one. He shot game and made camp in the shelter of a cliff dwelling the Indians had abandoned hundreds of years ago; he rode the length of Sonora and back, and when he finally trotted down the road into Bisbee he was dog-tired and still without a resolution of his troubles. He stabled the horse and walked stiffly up the square to the post office. Judge Williams, on his way out, nodded to him, but Santee gave no answer. He climbed the steps and hesitated at the door, looking across the Plaza. It was a hot and lonesome afternoon; there were few pedestrians in sight. At the door of the Turf Saloon he saw one proud beautiful shape, and that was Ellen Drury, watching the post office silently. Santee lifted his head, making a kind of vague signal of greeting, and the girl turned back inside the saloon. Very sober, Santee swung slowly inside and opened the door to Mossman's office.

Mossman looked up. He showed no surprise; he smiled a little, and said, "I hope you haven't forgiven me."

"No. I haven't."

"That's good," Mossman said. Santee couldn't figure him out. Mossman waved a hand. "Come on in. There's work to do."

"Does that mean I'm still on the payroll?"

"Nobody said anything about firing you."

"I see," Santee said. "Listen, soft soap won't work."

"I'm not apologizing. Get to work or quit—make up your mind, boy."

"All right," Santee said weakly, and shut the door behind him. "Don't you ever get scared?"

"Now and then," Mossman said abstractedly.

Santee shook his head; he felt uncomfortable; he said, "I'm going to get something to eat," and when Mossman made no response, he went outside, heading for the English Kitchen.

When he returned to the office Mossman was gone. Santee sat down and then remembered something, and went out to the stable to get his rifle off the saddle. He brought the rifle back inside the office, cleaned it and put it away in the rack. Then he sat down by the window in the dingy little office and used a short ramrod to run a cloth through the barrel of a revolver. *Chacon*, he thought. It always came back to Chacon. But it was Santee's conviction that Mossman was going far beyond bounds in his pursuit of Chacon.

Mossman entered the office and sat, and after a while spoke, "Do you know Billie Stiles and Burt Alvord?"

"I've seen them a few times," Santee answered. "Ran into them last winter at Maldonado's saloon in Washington Camp. Alvord took my gun. That was when I saw Chacon."

"Just so," Mossman murmured. Santee squinted down the revolver barrel, nodded with satisfaction and began loading .44 cartridges into the cylinder. He said, "What about those two?"

"If a message comes for me, from either one of them, you hop on your horse and find me, wherever I am."

Santee glanced up sharply. "Alvord and Stiles. Now, what would those two be doing sending you messages?"

"I've made a deal with them," Mossman said, and leaned forward over his desk, signing something.

Santee holstered the loaded gun and sat back, still puzzled. "What kind of deal?"

Mossman scribbled his bold signature across the last of the pile of letters, leaned his head back against the wall and looked past Santee, regarding the hills through the dusty window. "Alvord has a half-brother working down at the Minas Prietas in Sonora. I stopped by the mine last week on the way home and had a talk with the half-brother. I told him to get the word to Alvord that we'd do all we could to square him with the Arizona law, on one condition."

"Condition being Chacon," Santee said.

"Yes. I put a few drinks in Alvord's half-brother and

talked him into writing me a letter to Alvord. Then I rode up to Alvord's camp."

Santee knew better than to ask how Mossman had found the outlaw's camp. He only said, "You mean they let you in there, alone?"

"We had words," Mossman said. "I talked before they could start shooting, and I let them take my guns. They took me to Alvord. I showed him the letter and told him what we want. I told him I couldn't promise anything, but he could see that the Territory might be grateful to a man who helped capture Chacon. Alvord's got a wife in Prescott—and as things stand he can't see her."

"Good reasoning," Santee observed. "What'd he say?"

"He'll get together with Stiles and do what he can. I've worked out a plan. Colonel Greene has holding corrals at Naco, just this side of the Border. I've arranged with him to have a small herd of thoroughbred horses staked out there. Stiles is going to try and talk Chacon into crossing the Border with him to steal those thoroughbreds. Chacon doesn't know me by sight—we've never been face to face."

"What?"

"That's true," Mossman said, and went on smoothly. "If Stiles can talk him into this trap, I'll join the camp as one of Alvord's friends and ride across with them. As soon as we get Chacon on this side of the Border I'll take him."

"He won't fall for it."

"It's a chance."

Santee shook his head. "Hell, you hanged Drew in Mexico—why wait to get Chacon on this side of the Border?"

"I want him tried, convicted and hanged publicly."

"Why?"

"I want it made plain to all the thieves in the Territory that nobody can escape the Rangers."

"One man can't be all that important," Santee said.

"It's not the man. It's what he stands for. Chacon gets away with crime and laughs at the law. Our Mexicans think of him as a savior who's come to protect them by raiding the Anglos and punishing us for our so-called cruelties to their race."

"That ain't true."

"I know. Chacon's killed as many Mexicans as whites. But the truth isn't important. What's important is what the people believe. Chacon's raised a lot of heat between Anglos and Mexicans that was almost cooled down before he went on the warpath. He's given boys with a wild bent something to shoot for—he's a hero for all the toughs. We may run them down right and left, but as long as Chacon rides free, they look at him and say, 'If he can do it so can I.'"

"Sure," Santee said. "He's a star to follow. But I got into his camp and I found out what he's like, and I'll tell you something about him, Cap—I never heard anything as risky as this plan of yours. How do you know Stiles won't cross you? How can you trust Alvord? How do you know Chacon won't recognize you? How do you know anybody can talk him into this in the first place?"

"I don't."

Santee didn't answer. After a while he said in a thinner voice, "How long do you expect it'll take to set this up?"

"I don't know." Mossman was out of his chair by then, heading for the door.

"Where you going?"

"To take a ride. Mail those letters, will you?"

"Sure," Santee said. "You be gone long?"

"Can't say," Mossman said in a clipped manner. "I've had a report of Chacon up near Pearce. I thought I'd have a look. Probably a dead trail."

"Yeah," Santee breathed, and heard the door click shut behind Mossman. Mossman was either the nerviest man he had ever known, or the craziest. He knew for a fact that Mossman had been wrong, dead wrong, in hanging Jethro Drew. But he was beginning to understand the cause of Mossman's obsessive concentration on Augustin Chacon. He shook his head; he left his chair stiffly and crossed the room to fold the letters Mossman had left on the desk.

He sat in the dim, dusty office and glared with unfriendly eyes at the littered desk top before him. Work, for Santee at the time, consisted of the dry procedures of sorting out wanted posters and keeping the Rangers' paperwork up to date. He suspected the reason behind Mossman's taking him off the trail and confining him to the office, but he said nothing of it to anyone. Summer had blended into fall, August into September without change in routine. There had been no word from Alvord or Stiles. Behind the Rangers stood an impressively growing record of arrests and convictions, and an increasing unfriendliness toward the Rangers from the capitol at Phoenix; and never was Chacon sighted. Sick of it all, Santee cursed under his breath and swept papers into a pile, and swung impatiently out into the sunlit street. Mossman was out somewhere in the desert on one of his lonely rides, and might not return for a week. His rides usually resulted in the capture of some wanted man, greater or lesser, but every time Mossman returned to Bisbee his eyes were more haggard and his walk had a little less spring in it, and Chacon was still free.

Santee swung down the street with his hat tipped over his eyes, idly inspecting the town while he made his way across the intervening intersections to the makeshift hospital behind Padre Alejandro's church. There was a stiffness in his shoulder, the result of a bullet scratch he had suffered a week ago while capturing a pair of rustlers with Ranger Sergeant Dayton Graham; it had been the only time in the past weeks Mossman had allowed him out of the office. He came to the hospital today to have the dressing changed on the scabbed-over trench the slug had left in his flesh.

He met an antiseptic smell when he entered the low, raftered building. The windows were covered with thicknesses of oilpaper to keep out as much dust as possible. Lamps burned at intervals along the walls, and three yellow lanterns hung suspended from rafters in the center of the long room. A low moan issued from somewhere nearby. Santee had to pick his way past crowded cots. He came upon the doctor kneeling by a man with bandages wrapped around his torso—Dayton Graham, caught in an alley last week and knifed by three attackers. The doctor lifted a hand to Santee, making him wait. Santee nodded and watched Graham's face. Graham looked up at him; Santee could see the tracks of a week's steady pain in Graham's eyes. Graham said, "First chance I've had to loaf in a year."

The doctor spoke up in a half-cranky tone: "I don't mind you talking, Sergeant, but don't move around while I'm dressing this."

"Sorry," Graham said. When the doctor peeled the bandages back, Santee looked down. He had to turn his eyes away. Dayton Graham said, "It ain't that bad, Ranger. I've been hurt worse."

"And lived to tell about it," Santee said. "That's a wonder."

"It takes a rock-hard man to live to my age in our business, Santee."

The doctor glanced at Graham's face. "Stop moving around, damn it." Then he glanced at Santee. "Still cloudy outside?"

"The sun's showing through," Santee said. "But I think it'll rain before nightfall."

"We need a wetting-down to settle the dust," the doctor said. "Sergeant, when this heals over, you'll be a walking mass of scar tissue. My advice is that you find a quieter line of work."

"Too late for that," Graham said. "There hasn't been a day since I grew up when I haven't had a gun in my hand."

"The day's coming when none of us will need guns," the doctor said.

"I hope so," Graham answered. "But it'll be awhile yet, Doctor. The streets still need shotguns."

The doctor tied the last gauze strip in place and stood up. In his shirt, with the sleeves rolled up past his elbows, he was gaunt and angular. The overhead lamp cast sharp shadows across his craggy face. "All I can do is patch," he said. "I can't replace torn-up muscles. From this point on, Sergeant, you'll have to live with less activity—or not at all."

"I've hurt too many men," Graham said. "I can't afford

to relax now, Doctor. But I've got no regrets. I've lived long past my time."

"Then be careful," the doctor said, and turned to Santee. "Come along, Ranger." He threaded his way past jumbled cots, most of them occupied, into the little room beyond the end of the ward, where medicines were kept. Santee said: "You look busy. Maybe I ought to come back another time."

"I'm always busy," the doctor said. "This country's hard on flesh and bones. You're here now, Ranger—let's see that cut."

Santee unbuttoned his shirt and pushed it gently back from his shoulder. The doctor lifted the bandage enough to peer underneath, and stepped back with a nod. "It's all scabbed now. I'd keep the bandage on for another day or two, to avoid the chance of hitting it on something and breaking it open again."

"All right," Santee said. "Doctor—how bad is it with the Sergeant?"

"Worse than he thinks." The doctor grunted and turned his back to gather some medicines on a shelf. "He ought to spend his time in a rocking chair with his memories. God knows he's got enough of them."

"And not much else," Santee said, a little drily.

"No. This isn't a rewarding occupation you're in."

"I think about that," Santee said, "from time to time."

"Then why stay with it?"

Santee shook his head. "A man gives you a job. You do it."

"Just bread and wine, then?"

"I reckon it's more than that," Santee said. "But for sure it ain't glory. Ain't no glory in ending up buried under a rockpile out in the hills, with nobody to cry over you but a coyote. And it ain't to get rich. You think about it too much, I guess, and you start knowing it takes a damn fool to get into this business. Maybe it's just that somebody asked me to do it."

"Mossman?"

"Yes."

"Loyalty, then," the doctor suggested.

"I don't know as you'd call it that," Santee said. "You want to know the truth, I don't spend a whole lot of time thinkin' about it. I'd probably quit if I did."

"Perhaps all of us would quit," the doctor said, and turned into the ward with a tray of bottles and steel tools. "Wash that shoulder with soap and water as often as you can. The stiffness will last a few more days."

"Yeah," Santee said. "Much obliged." He went by the tangle of patients' cots and paused by the door, nodding to Dayton Graham, flat on his back. After a moment's consideration he dropped a dollar in the poorbox and went outside. The clouds had closed up again and the afternoon was gray and cool with a touch of dampness in the air, promising rain. He cruised the walks without purpose for a while, reluctant to return to the deadliness of paperwork. He came into the Plaza and paused at the door of the Turf Saloon to light a cigar. Standing before the open-top doorway, he felt the stale weight of tobacco smoke and the bored drone of voices rolling at him. With several unimportant, unconnected thoughts idling past his mind, he pushed inside and made a place at the bar. He swept the room with a casual glance, after which he accepted a mug of beer and cruised around the saloon seeking an empty chair. Near the front of the room he found a place near Ellen Drury's roulette table, and sat, looking across a short distance at the woman's profile. No one was playing at her game at the moment; she turned, and Santee said, "Howdy, Miss Drury."

She nodded to him. "How are you, Santee?"

"So-so," he answered. "Ain't seen such a dull day in years."

"There's always excitement enough for a man looking for it," she said. She came idly around her table and sat down near him, surveying the saloon with a blank glance something akin to Mossman's customary look. She said, "I hear you and Sergeant Graham found a little excitement last week."

"I reckon," Santee muttered.

The woman gave him a little sardonic look and picked up a discarded newspaper from the table where Santee's arm lay with his drink. "Have a look," she said, pushing the newspaper toward him. "They've just sworn in Roosevelt as President. McKinley's assassin goes on trial next week. Isn't that excitement, Santee?"

"Three thousand miles away," Santee said. "What difference does it make to us?"

"Roosevelt may appoint a new governor for Arizona," she said, speaking softly, vaguely; there was a faraway light in her glance. "That might affect your company."

Santee gave it a moment's thought. "I suppose it could. But I ain't seen any new governor yet."

"One of the ignorant Rough Riders, I've heard," Ellen Drury murmured. A man wandered up to stand by the green roulette layout, and she went back to spin the wheel. Santee finished the last swallow of his beer, nodded to the woman, and left the table with no destination in mind.

"CAP!"

When he left the saloon his aimless walk took him in the direction of Angius's store, and it was purely by accident that his eyes happened to glance in through the window. What he saw inside arrested him abruptly. He stood uncertain in the commencing drizzle, looking in. Nothing seemed amiss; yet there was something about the attitude of the man at the drygoods counter that held Santee's attention. That man had his back to Santee, and his pose seemed strange—his shoulders were hunched up and his head was lowered, as if in heavy, defensive concentration. Beyond that man, Santee could see Angius, standing on the far side of the counter with an intense frown on his face and his body absolutely motionless. Rain dripped gray before Santee's face. Suspicious of the static scene before him, he turned the doorknob and stepped inside.

"Everything all right, Mr. Angius?"

"Smith!" Angius said; and that was all.

The man between them whirled, snapping his head around, and Santee had a brief positive look at the square, lean jaw, the dark overhanging brows and the eyes, triangular like a snake's. That man's lips were pulled back in a deadly grin, showing a row of glistening teeth; there was a gun lifting in his hand. Santee said, "Chacon!" and closed his hand around his gun butt.

He knew he was going to be too late; he saw Chacon's pistol coming to bear, and his thoughts whirled in frenzy: *God, make him miss!*

But Chacon did not miss. With his gun half raised, Santee felt the bullet jar his body. He winked dismally at Chacon; he felt himself falling, he felt himself dying; and he said, "Cap—Cap!"

CHAPTER XII

GOVERNOR'S MEMORIES

"Six, seven, eight." Judge Williams paused at the top of the capitol steps to look at the angry clouds covering the southern half of the sky. The cold, hostile capitol building yawned before him and he settled his shoulders stiffly before he advanced into the hall, walking through to the outer executive office. He thought, *What next, I wonder?* The sallow clerk nodded to him with funereal silence and indicated that he should sit down. "How is he?" the judge asked.

"All right," the clerk told him; it would be only a moment; and the clerk disappeared. Judge Williams settled his length into a maroon leather chair, and, as he had done many a time, let his eyes travel along the withdrawn spareness of the room. This day was to mark the end of a significant period of Arizona's history; he recognized the fact with some little awe, and wondered again what changes the future would make.

He lifted his head when E. S. Ives and Colonel Epes Randolph entered the room together; he nodded to them and watched them sit down. No one spoke. Judge Williams shifted his seat and lit his pipe. Several minutes later Colonel Randolph said softly: "A sad day. Even you must admit it's a sad day, my friend."

"Yes," Ives said, "yes."

It wasn't long before the clerk reappeared at the end of the room, standing aside to hold the big door open. "All right, gentlemen."

Judge Williams felt a certain discomfort as he stepped through the door behind Ives. Everything was as it had always been; yet over it all hung the atmosphere of sadness, mixed with a regretful and quiet anger. Governor Murphy sat in his high wooden chair behind the desk, with his back to the wide window through which the judge could see the cloudy sky over misty mountain peaks. The Governor's stubby-fingered hands lay clasped over the expanse of his stomach and his chin rested upon his chest. He did not speak until the judge had entered the room and shut the heavy door, and taken a seat. The weight of uncertain health, personal loss and political disaster—all these things hung over the governor; yet his shoulders were not lowered and his face did not sag. Judge Williams felt a sudden rush of admiration, a sudden profound sympathy. He saw the others pulling chairs forward and seating themselves, and he pulled his own chair up.

Only then did the governor speak, with gruff resonance: "I'm deeply pleased you all could come."

"We'd have been bastards not to," Ives said gently.

"Coming from you," the governor said to Ives, "that's a compliment not to be ignored. You ought to know that I respect you equally, old friend."

"You don't have to tell me that."

The governor nodded and straightened, putting his elbows on the top of the desk, laying his arms forward. "We'd best get down to business, then. This is a busy day for me. There are a great many things to be prepared. I asked you three here partly for sentimental reasons, and partly to ask you a last favor. First, a personal reason. One of the greatest, most moving experiences of my life has been to work with you men in thrusting progress forward throughout this Territory. If a man's wealth can be measured in the number and quality of his friends, then I must consider myself wealthy. We've had a good time, all of us—we've all learned a great deal from our association, and my greatest single regret is that all this will not be permitted to continue. I'd have accomplished nothing without you, and I might have accomplished too many wrong things without some of you to keep me in hand. I find it impossible to—"

"We all know our limitations, Governor," Epes Randolph said. "I think we've worked and fought enough so that we all know what our mutual feelings are. We know your meaning perfectly—spare yourself the embarrassment of going on."

The governor nodded in a gesture of humility. "Thank you."

Then his wide face moved and Judge Williams caught once more a glimpse of the old light in his eyes. The governor said, in a stronger tone, "In that case, let's get to business, shall we?"

He rose and pushed his chair aside, and stood at his desk with his hands folded behind him and his head lifted. "Today is my last official day in office. The Administration has seen fit to replace me with a new man, Major Brodie of the Rough Riders. Whether this is good or not is, of course, not for us to judge. We might accuse the Major of accepting the governorship as a political reward; but I must remember that I accepted the same job in the same way. We might accuse him of being a stranger, unacquainted with our problems. But I was a stranger here once, too. If the Territory will have gained from either of us, it must consider itself fortunate.

"You'll agree, I think, that we've initiated several programs, or expanded existing ones, that will assuredly benefit Arizona if they're encouraged to continue. Among others I might mention the system of public schools, the establishment of the Rangers as a Territorial police force, our liberal policies toward Mexican and Indian citizens, and the growth of the university at Tucson. There are a great many others but you all know what they are and there's not much point in belaboring them now."

The governor turned heavily, walking to the window, and stood there silently over a stretching period before he returned to his desk and stood with one hand lowered to its rim. His eyes swept the group. "The favor I have to ask of you is that you use all the influence at your command with Governor Brodie, to persuade him to continue these programs. I wouldn't ask this of you if I had any clear idea of what he's got in mind to do, but I know nothing of his opinions and I think it's necessary that we impress upon him the importance of continuing Arizona's growth. He's got to make use of the programs we've already begun. They've proved more than satisfactory. If he doesn't—"

The governor paused long enough to study each man's face. Judge Williams felt the pressure of his insistent glance. Governor Murphy said, "Will you do this for me? Epes?"

"Of course," Colonel Randolph said. "Major Brodie doesn't know this part of the country well. We shouldn't have too hard a time persuading him to continue what we've started."

The governor nodded and turned to Ives, who said slowly: "I'm afraid I'll have to wait and see what Brodie has in mind. But so long as he doesn't produce any ideas better than what we've already got, I owe it to you to agree."

"I'm obliged," the governor said. "And you, Starr?"

"It's an insult that you should feel the need to ask me," Judge Williams said. "It's really a silly damned question. We'll all do as much as we can to keep the new man in line, just as we did with you. You didn't have to ask it."

"I know." The governor bowed his head with a gentle smile. "But vanity required that I enlist your verbal support. Memories of things like this will be all I'll have left after tomorrow."

"Governor," Colonel Randolph said, "where do you go from here?"

"I haven't decided," the governor said. To Judge Williams it seemed that the governor was convinced he should reserve his decision until after everything here was over. It was typical of Murphy. The personal must always come after the political. In that quality Judge Williams found a distinct similarity between Governor Murphy and Captain Burt Mossman, in spite of Mossman's avowed self-interest; and he wondered that he hadn't seen the likeness of their separate dedications before.

The governor pulled his chair forward, about to sit down, but he did not sit; he said in a businesslike way: "That's all, then. The meeting's ended. I'll call on you all in the next few days. And one thing—you cannot imagine the depth of my gratitude to all of you. Starr, can you stay a moment?"

Judge Willams nodded and kept his seat while the others came forward solemnly to shake Governor Murphy's hand. Colonel Randolph spoke a few words; the governor dipped his head; Randolph turned and left. When the door closed behind Ives, Judge Williams saw the governor sit down and slump slowly deeper into his chair, growing at once smaller and heavier before him.

"Starr," the governor said, "I'm done. I'm washed out."

"Nervous energy lasts only so long," the judge said. "I'd imagine with a little rest you'll be back on your feet. You've done a mammoth task."

Governor Murphy's head moved slowly back and forth. "Not just rest, Starr. I don't think so. I really don't."

Judge Williams snorted with more assurance than he felt. "You're tough as a mustang."

With visible effort the governor pulled himself forward to lean his elbows on the desk top. He looked wretchedly tired. The judge was amazed that the man had been able to conceal all this so well during the gathering just past. The governor said, "Starr, I appreciate your confidence in my health, and your flattery, but that isn't why I asked you to stay. I have an additional favor to ask of you."

"Ask it."

"It has to do with Burt."

The judge nodded, "I thought it would come around to that."

"I believe you've come to know him better than any of the rest of us, Starr. I've left this to you."

"Go on."

"I've talked with him recently. I find it confounded difficult to reach the man—he seals himself up as effectively as a caterpillar in a cocoon."

"Yes," Judge Williams said.

"I'm worried about him. We're in a ticklish situation where he's concerned. I've already been formally notified that he's to be replaced. A Sergeant Rynning from Major Brodie's unit is to assume the captaincy of the Rangers."

The judge lowered his face. "I'm sorry to hear that," he murmured. "Deeply sorry. Burt's been a powerful force."

"Perhaps too powerful. I've appealed the appointment of Rynning, but I've been turned down. Burt was here a few days ago and I told him he'd have to submit his resignation."

"And he refused?"

"No. No, of course not. I have his resignation right here. It becomes effective the first of the month. He was most gracious about it."

"Then what's troubling you?"

"Ever since he took the job," the governor said, "he's had a single overpowering goal, more important than all his other missions."

"Augustin Chacon."

"Just so. Chacon has become an obsession with Burt—especially since Chacon killed one of Burt's top men in Angius's store in Bisbee. I'm afraid of that obsession, Starr."

"Why?"

"Because, for one thing, it may become the ruin of him."

"How?"

"Suppose he hasn't tracked down Chacon by the first of the month. You concede that's probable?"

"Yes," the judge said. "Of course."

"Then suppose Mossman decides to take the law into his own hands when he reverts to being a civilian."

"He holds a deputy U.S. Marshal's commission, doesn't he?"

"That's worthless," the governor said. "Chacon isn't wanted for federal offenses. But let's suppose Burt continues this hunt alone."

"Suppose he does," the judge returned.

"It could do great harm to Arizona."

"How?"

"According to Burt," the governor said, "Chacon is now in Mexico, and has been for some time. Suppose, as a private citizen, Burt captures him in Mexico and brings him across the Border."

"It seems to me," Judge Williams observed, "that you sanctioned something like that not too long ago. As I remember, you told me you'd take full responsibility—

and you said you had an arrangement with Colonel Kosterlitzky of the Rurales."

"This isn't the same thing. Burt will have no official connection with our government after the first of the month—that's only ten days from now. I doubt he can expect any help or even leniency from the new governor. Starr, if Burt does what I'm afraid of, it will be a plain case of an American citizen kidnapping a Mexican citizen on Mexican soil. The complications could be disastrous. The Legislature's on the brink now. All it will take will be one foolish move like this, and they'll disband the Rangers."

"Not if Mossman's no longer a Ranger."

"His action will still reflect on the Rangers."

"Perhaps it will," the judge conceded, "if he really does what you suspect."

"It could also send Burt to jail," the governor said quietly. "That would break him. I know he wouldn't be able to take it. It would kill him. He's a free soul—as individual as any man alive. Unfortunately that's one of his greatest weaknesses, as well as a strength. In government administrative work we can have no more privacy than life in a goldfish bowl will permit. There are a great many things our consciences would ordinarily let us do, as personal matters. But these are acts we can't allow ourselves, just because if we commit them, we're holding up an image to the public that the public's moral sense dislikes. Burt doesn't care about public opinion. It doesn't affect him—he thinks. But public opinion can railroad a man straight to prison if the circumstances are right. Now, I've seen in this obsession of Burt's certain indications—hints that if he's left to follow his own inclinations, he may do things that can't be considered prudent or sensible. If he were just another tough with a gun, it would be one thing. But he's not. In his position, even if he's technically an ex-Ranger, a private citizen, he'll be unavoidably associated with the Rangers, and by the same token he'll be connected with me and our policies. What he does reflects on our whole system, since by association he's a representative of it. Any violence he commits will tend to characterize all of us in the eyes of the new administration. That's why we can't afford to let him go berserk."

"That's a strong word," Judge Williams said.

"I'm afraid it's none too strong. It frightens me, Starr, to watch him—if he does anything to turn Brodie against our policies, we'll have lost a great many years of effort."

The governor tilted his head to rest it against the high back of his chair. "And there's one other thing. I like Burt. I admire him. He's a gentleman and he's got all the self-respect and pride that we all wish we had. He takes the same chances as any man who lives by the sword, but if there's anything I can do to prevent it, I won't see him destroyed by his own hand. I like him too much, Starr."

"So do I," the judge said, "confound it. What do you want me to do?"

"Talk to him. I believe he's in Tucson, tidying up his affairs and getting provisions to take up Chacon's trail again. Somehow, Starr, we've got to impress him with the importance of what he sees as mere technicalities. He's too good a man."

Judge Williams nodded and stood. "I'll see what I can do," he said.

CHAPTER XIII

INSCRUTABLE MAN

Late in the cool evening he stepped off the stagecoach at the Tucson depot and looked up and down Congress Street, wondering where he should begin his search. He decided on the simplest method, and went around to the police station, leaving word that when Mossman was found he should be informed that Judge Williams wished to see him. Thereafter the judge went to the hotel a block away and made his presence known by going into the dining room and staying there, looking out through the window, watching life in the Old Pueblo. Tucson was a large and bustling town with a good deal of commerce moving along the streets. Lamps bloomed out of windows and doorways, illuminating Congress Street outside. Above yonder rooftops, the moon played strangely on a few clouds to the south. The judge had his supper and then sat back, glancing around the room. It was a gaudy room dominated by gaudy chandeliers and a gaudy bright-colored stone fireplace, above which hung a brown-barreled, exquisitely engraved Kentucky flintlock rifle. The judge's appreciative eye followed the line of carving forward from the flint-hammer lockplate to the front of the breech, and back again along the meticulously decorated wood stock. He devoted a moment's thought to those men who devoted lifetimes to the beautification of weapons of death—swords, clubs, knives, rifles, pistols, shotguns. He shook his head and turned away from the fireplace in time to see Burt Mossman's small, powerful figure coming across the room. Mossman shook his hand and brought up a chair saying, "I was on my way back to Bisbee."

"I know. I wanted to see you first." The judge put his grave glance on Mossman and contemplated the ways in which he might open the conversation. Across the table, Mossman sat quite relaxed and extracted a thick cigar from his vest pocket; he lit it with a wooden match and tossed the match into the fireplace a few feet away, and waited politely.

"Dayton Graham told me," the judge began, "that once your resignation becomes effective, you'll be leaving the Territory."

"Yes."

"Why?"

Mossman's eyelids lifted for an instant. Judge Williams saw a brief streak of questioning brightness, and then the eyelids dropped again. Mossman said, "I've some work to do with Bill Greene in Kansas." Mossman tapped ash from his cigar into his open hand; he held it that way for a moment, then moved to toss the ashes into the fire. It occurred to Judge Williams that Mossman's solemnity was huge and unbreakable; the man's strict reserve was held by constantly close guard. From the attitude of Mossman's body, dropped into the chair as it was, Judge Williams decided that the man's pose of loose weariness was not a truthful one. Mossman was too plainly on his defenses. But there was no time to go around; the judge said, "What about Chacon, Burt?"

"What about Chacon?" Mossman murmured in reply, and glanced at him with sleepy eyes. Judge Williams thought there was something almost unfriendly in Mossman's tone, but he let it pass and presently forgot about it. Mossman's face remained impassive and when he replied the judge heard no further touch of irritation.

"A good many people have baited me with that question, Starr. The only answer I've got is that he will be run down. Eventually all mad dogs are run down."

"You put that impersonally," Judge Williams said. "Do you mean the law will run him down, or do you mean you'll run him down?"

"Whichever of us gets to him first," Mossman said in a low tone.

"Then you no longer consider yourself the law."

"Not after the end of this month. How can I?"

"If you can't, why must you continue this feud?"

Mossman's head tipped up. For a moment the judge almost thought he was going to see an outburst; but Mossman only regarded him with blank politeness, and he could no longer find the slight hint of explosiveness that he had seen momentarily in Mossman's face. Mossman stood up and tapped his cigar into the fire, and then paused there to reach up. He had to stand on tiptoe to grasp the Kentucky rifle. He lifted it from its rack and took it down, and eared the flinted hammer back. A pair of clicks, crisp and loud, echoed against the judge's ears. Mossman sighted along the barrel in an idle way, aiming into the fire, and spoke suddenly:

"I don't mean to seem unreasonable, Starr, and I don't really consider this a feud—up till a few weeks ago I hadn't reduced it to the level of a personal vendetta. But then he killed my best man, and one of the most worthwhile men I've ever met."

The judge said nothing. Mossman let the rifle's hammer down gently and turned to replace the long weapon on its rack. Then he stayed by the fire, talking slowly: "The fact seems clear that as long as Chacon's allowed free, death and grief will keep littering his path. He's got to be stopped. I take it on myself to stop him for a number of reasons. First, and most obviously, he's killed Santee. Second, he's escaped me altogether too many times. It's become almost an affront to me—I can't help feeling that all this time he's been laughing at me."

"You don't like being laughed at, do you, Burt?"

"No. But I've got other reasons. I took a job. My work will have failed if Chacon stays free. And here's another thing: by this time I've come to know him better than any man alive. I know his habits. I know half the hideouts he uses and three quarters of the trails he follows. I've been right behind him for so many months that I'm almost beginning to be able to think the way he thinks. If there's a man in this country with any chance at all of running down Chacon, I'm that man. Then again, I've enlisted the help of two men below the Border who may be able to lead him into a trap I've devised. So you see I can't quit him now, Starr—whether or not I carry a badge."

Mossman tossed his cigar in the fire and returned to his chair, where before long he lit another cigar and leaned one arm against the table. He put his glance on the judge and in that brief, broken instant, Judge Williams thought he saw something else: Mossman's pride had been rubbed more than he had admitted. Pride, the judge suddenly decided, was what pushed Burt Mossman; pride was what kept him on the track of the outlaw. The rest was superfluous. It showed, or so it seemed to Judge Williams, in slight signs—the drawn tautness ground into the expression around Mossman's lips and eyes; the carefully cut fawn-brown suit he wore; the aloof barrier surrounding him. Judge Williams sat with these thoughts and began to feel irritated by Mossman's supreme air of rightness—an air without piety, but allowing no question.

Mossman touched the points of his mustache with thumb and forefinger, and inserted his cigar between his lips. He rolled his shoulders forward, leaning both arms on the table. He said: "Chacon will come down, Starr. I've made myself that promise."

"Be careful of the way he comes down. Be careful he doesn't bring you down with him."

"We all take that chance."

"I'm not talking about the chance of dying. I mean the chance of being destroyed—not physically."

"Make your point," Mossman said gently.

"If you allow this hunt to drive everything else from your mind, you become no better than he is."

"I don't agree," Mossman said. "The only chance I have of catching him is to pursue his trail with single-minded purpose."

"You make yourself into a manhunting machine, then—no more."

"Perhaps that's all I've ever been."

"No. Of course not. I've seen a great deal more than that in you. I've seen it, Burt, but I don't see it now. A man's more than a mechanism to pull a trigger."

Mossman shook his head. "A gun's a tool, no better and no worse than the man holding it. It's always a mistake to condemn weapons, Starr. It's not weapons that hurt men. It's other men. And my experience has been that only one man with a gun can stop another man with a gun. There's no other way; it all comes down to that, just that simply."

"Maybe it does," the judge said reluctantly. "But how can we be so certain who's the man to be stopped?"

"Look at Chacon."

"Granted, he's your bad one. But still when you descend to his level, with no more authority than any other private citizen, then you become no better than Chacon—and in that case, you've got two men shooting at each other and the outcome will make no difference. It won't solve anything. Don't let it happen, Burt—don't let yourself fall."

"Murphy put you up to this," Mossman said quietly, with a bit of a smile.

"I won't deny that."

"Murphy's a hell of a good man," Mossman murmured. "So are you, Starr. But so was Santee Smith." He stood up, crushing out his cigar. "I've always tried to conduct myself with honor, Starr. Not for anyone's benefit but my own. And nothing's changed. You've done your duty by the governor, and I thank you. I've got to assemble some supplies, and I'm taking an early train."

"Nothing I can say will stop you?"

"Nothing. I wish you wouldn't try—I don't want to see you beg, Starr."

"I won't beg for my life," Judge Williams said. "But I'll beg for yours."

"It's mine to do with as I see fit."

Judge Williams moved his head from side to side; but he rose and took Mossman's hand, and held it, and then watched Mossman's bantam shape retreat from the room. Then, for a long while, he stared into the wavering fire; it had at last come to him that what blinded Mossman was his own overstrict code of personal morality. Nothing that the judge knew of would change that. His eyes lifted to the mantel, and the long rifle above it. Part blinded by having stared into the fire, he considered the hazy outline of the Kentucky flintlock and heard in the room around him men's voices running softly through the air; he shook his head once more, and went away from the table.

CHAPTER XIV

A PROUD FAREWELL

She waited in his hotel room until he came; she caught hold of his glance and held it. Presently he closed the door behind him and stood by the door with the lamplight changing his features strangely, and said, "This isn't smart."

"I know," she said. "But you didn't intend to come back to Bisbee, did you?"

"As a matter of fact, I did."

"Then you didn't intend to see me."

"No," he said. "I didn't."

She sat in the chair, quite still; after a while she said, "Sit down, damn it."

She had the only chair. He went to the bed and sat, and tugged off his boots. She knew he wasn't making a point of ignoring her; it was just that her presence wasn't as important to him as she wanted it to be. She said, "I make a good piece of furniture, don't I?"

He tossed his boot on the floor and hitched himself up on the bed with his legs stretched out and his torso sitting up against the iron bedstead. He said, "You don't look quite the same as you look in your house on the hill."

"Ah," she said. "Then the house does matter after all."

"No. It isn't the house. It's a change in you."

She looked away. "I suppose you're right. I lose some of my self-certainty away from the house. I shouldn't do that, should I?"

"Don't ask me to give you advice."

"No," she said, rebuffed. "I'm sorry." His curtness to-night troubled her. He was a man of pride, but all men were men of pride; the difference was, to her, that his was not an unreasoning pride. She hated the assumption in most men that they owned a greater strength than hers, a greater wisdom; she hated their masks of wise tolerance, hiding insincerity and hypocrisy. But Mossman's pride was a product of his reason; his mask was a mask of hard, personal intolerance; his eyes were always shrewd, always a little cruel. She could not treat him with the kind of insolence she used to defend herself against the others. Yet she could not put on a front of cool contempt or gray pessimism. She could put on no front at all, she could only offer what she was; and he did not seem to want it.

Watching his motionless form on the bed, she felt a little bitterness, and knew that part of it came from the knowledge that she was the same as other women; she owned desires that this man could command, and it made her feel weak. She needed her independence; he would not give it to her, yet he would not take it from her. She said: "It would be comforting if I could hate you. But I can't escape myself."

"It would be best," he answered, "if you could forget me. I won't be back."

"I'll follow you, then."

"No."

He had not threatened her; yet his single word stopped her cold in her tracks. He had forbidden her; she could not follow him. "Damn," she said. "Damn. Why did this happen?"

"Because you let it happen."

"Yes," she said. "I should have had the sense."

He lit a cigar, and reached his arm out to draw the porcelain washbasin closer along the top of the desk, so that he could use it for his ashes. He said, "Do you mind if I tell you something about yourself?"

"I don't mind. Tell me."

"You met a man," he said, "who thinks the way you'd like to be able to think. He fits into a pattern you've been trying to mold for yourself. He seems to have the answers you've been searching for. He knows the reason—he is the reason. He knows the meaning; he is the meaning. You've got enough sense to know he's right. But you make a mistake when you try to change yourself to become like him. It would be better to take yourself as you are and work from that, than to change yourself—because you really can't change yourself. You're only putting up a disguise. You're a woman in raw country, and you think you've found your defense against it—but you can't use me, or your money, or your house, or anything else external, as a defense. You've got to make use of yourself. You've got to be able to fight your own fights, or else adjust."

"And if I adjust, I'm admitting I've failed."

"Yes."

"You're right, of course," she said. "That's the answer to the whole thing—all of it but one part."

"What's that?"

"I can't change my emotions," she said.

He snubbed his cigar out. "I'm sorry about that. I can't do anything for you."

"It's funny," she said. "Any other man would have to offer me more than he could ever own, for the same thing I'd give to you in exchange for a word."

"I won't speak that word," he said. "Perhaps that's why you feel free to make the offer."

"Could that be it?" she said. "Damn it, Mossman, I wish I knew the answer." She rose from the chair; she said: "Dayton Graham was right. I'd have been better off if I'd never met you. My life would be happier. But I have no regrets. Goodbye, Mossman."

"Goodbye," he said.

She left the room and went forward along the hall to the lobby; she went out in the street and down to the livery stable, and picked up her buggy, and drove out of town southeastward under a beginning drizzle and a black cavernous sky.

CHAPTER XV

TRAIL OF THE OUTLAW

Mossman awoke and looked to his window, and saw the gray gloom of morning rain. On the roof it rattled like gravel. "A day that dies before it's born," he murmured, and moved to get out of bed. He washed and shaved with efficient speed and donned a set of well worn range clothes—Justin boots, patched Levis, a flannel shirt, a bearskin coat and flop-brimmed, sweat-stained hat. Over the outside of the thick coat he buckled his heavy gun belt, letting the revolver in its flap-holster sag against his hip. Then, with a bandanna tied about his throat, and a pair of fur-lined gloves stuffed under his gun belt, he dumped half a box of .45 shells in his pocket and was ready. He went up the street through the rain to the Southern Pacific depot, Colonel Epes Randolph's outfit, and carried his saddlebags inside. He ate a box lunch there, washing it down with tepid coffee, and boarded the six-fifty train for Douglas. The morning was damply cold.

He stepped into the crowded Pullman car and took a seat. Up ahead, four cowboys in opposite seats upended a suitcase in the middle of the aisle to play poker. The car soon became steamy, too still and too warm and too smoky. The train lurched forward and left Tucson on time, clattering out over the desert roadbed. A wrangler with horse stench strong on his clothes shared Mossman's seat. Whiskey odor rode on that one's breath and he lay sound asleep, his head rocking back and forth against the seat. Bunches of greasewood and mesquite and cat's-claw spun by on the edge of the roadbed. Mossman stood up and climbed past the drunk wrangler to walk out onto the open, swaying platform between cars; he stood there with rain droplets and wind whipping his sun-dry skin. The rumbling clack-clack of iron wheels made him fall into a half-sleep; he leaned against the railing and braced his legs.

Beyond the whirling scrubs and trees, he watched the ragged edges of nearby hills, dimly visible through the rain, and he felt vaguely, remotely disappointed. The train ran forward into the thicker depth of the storm until he was surrounded by leaking blackness; he could see neither foreground nor sky. It was as though the earth had dropped away and he was alone on a train rushing through an endless rainy night, with no beginning and no particular direction. The wind was cold; melancholy uncertainties made him turn to the soggy warmth of the car and go back to his seat.

An uneven rail splice made the car rock and rumble. Penny-sized blobs of water moved slowly backward along the outside of the windowpane. Mossman tilted his head back against the corner of the seat and closed his eyes, and his mind. The whiskey odor on the wrangler's breath was thick and soporific.

When the train swayed to a halt in Douglas it had left the storm a long way behind; it was noon and the sky was cloudy but not raining. Mossman walked across the cinder platform, over a succession of streets and into the damp, dim interior of the adobe livery barn. He picked up the horse he had left here, paid the hostler, saddled up and tied his blanket roll and saddlebags onto concho strings before he stepped up and rode away southward, toward the clouds, toward Mexico.

The muzzle of his Winchester erupted in a round, dry tone that crashed in undulating echo patterns across the rock-strewn gullies. Down below, on the point of his aim, he saw dust jump from the strike of his bullet against a jackrabbit's fur. He cursed mildly because there was no better game in these hills; he stood up, rammed the Winchester into his saddle boot and swung up into the saddle. The sun was almost down, glaring brassy red through a small hole in the solid cloud blanket. He leaned far back in the saddle and gigged the horse down the steep slope, and a hundred yards later dismounted with his knife to skin the dead rabbit.

He was careful to build a smokeless fire; and by the time the last light drained out of the evening, the fire was put out and he had moved a quarter-mile up the gully to make his dry camp for the night. It was bitter cold. This was Chacon country and he didn't want to make his presence known. There was a thin chance someone might have heard his rifle shot; but if anyone had heard it, and was hostile to him, he knew better than to camp near his fire.

Before dawn he was in the saddle, bearskin coat buckled to his throat; it had been a bitter night and he knew it would take hours to work the chill from his body. He blew on his hands and slipped them into his gloves, and buckled down the angora chaps to protect his legs as much as he could. As late as ten o'clock he felt the bite of the day's curt air; but shortly thereafter he descended a steep and looping game trail that dropped him a quick thousand feet almost to the floor of the desert, and the temperature rose sharply. He wheeled off the last hillside and ran up the trough of a shallow arroyo a short distance, and came out onto the plain; he glanced up at the steel-brittle clouds and hunched his collar higher against the back of his neck, feeling a chill that was not altogether in the weather down here.

The mountains fell behind. He slowed the horse's pace when he topped a scrub-covered hill. Beyond that summit he had seen the heavy smoke spiral of a campfire, and so he halted in a grove of red-branch manzanita, pulled his army telescope from the saddlebag, and had a long, steady look through it.

"Cow camp," he murmured, holding the 'scope up. "The Cananea outfit. Four vaqueros—none of them anyone I want. Let's keep on."

He collapsed the 'scope and replaced it, and lifted his reins. His chosen path took him in a southwesterly direction, pressing steadily deeper into the chain of rugged mountains along the Mexican side of the Border. It was in this region that he had last caught sight of Chacon, and it was here that he must resume his search. His cigar smoke streaked away thinly on the breeze.

In midafternoon he dropped along a timbered mountainside into a dry riverbed and turned downstream in the center of it. Loose gravel reported the crush of the horse's hoofs. Five days ago Chacon had camped here; Mossman had come this close before weather and lack of supplies had forced him to turn back to Naco. Now he searched the shadowed boulder pockets for sign, and at last came upon the long-dead ashes of Chacon's fire. Careful inspection produced a grunt from his chest: Chacon must have doubled back, for there were signs of two camps here, one of them not more than twenty-four hours old, and the double sign of horse tracks showed that the same pony, with a chipped off-front shoe, had been here both times. His eyes opened a little wider and his hand closed around the butt of his big revolver. There was no way to be certain that Chacon wasn't somewhere in the trees immediately above him, looking down and distending his lips in long, silent laughter. Mossman settled his shoulders; his jaw crept forward to lie in a strong line.

A broken-edged twig here, a white-scraped rock there, an occasional vague hoofprint in sand or dark soil—these vague and sporadic signs made it possible for him to ride forward on the outlaw's trail as though it had been painted before him with a bright, broad stripe. The track took him out of the riverbed and on through the cool high passes. Flakes of snow, crisp and light, touched his cheeks; it was already dead winter up here. The wind whipped his coat collar up against his face and fluttered snow against his eyelids, and even with gloved hands and legs protected by the thickness of the angora chaps, he felt the strike of the unfriendly mountain weather. Snow fell around him in loose piles; it came down to coat his hat and his horse; the weight of it increased, and the falling thickness, and by sundown he knew he would have to quit for the night and find shelter.

The intermittent signs had brought him, by a round-about and seemingly unhurried route, to a sagging stone cabin sheltered by the steep wall of a limestone cliff. The old cabin stood like a stone pillar, a forgotten gray monument to its builder, slightly cocked to one side. A month ago Mossman had passed by here and received a cup of coffee from a roaming horse-hunter who had been making his headquarters here. He hoped the old man would still be here; but as he made his careful approach, he found no visible signs of horses or human occupation nearby, and had to assume the old place was abandoned.

With his rifle ready, he dismounted by the cabin and pushed the warped door aside with his boot. After a brief silence he whirled inside and took a quick sweeping survey; but no one was present. He frowned and looked around more carefully; his eyes rode from point to point, taking in detail: the ashes of a fire in the open stove; the table made of split aspen trunks; the oil lamp rusting on a shelf; the woodbox half full by the stove; racks beside the doorway with hats and spurs and ropes and hackamores suspended from them; an aspen-frame armchair with its seat of buckskin leather, laced with dried rawhide; a littered pile of saddles, bridles and ropes lying tangled in one corner, with the snout of a rifle poking through; water bucket and ash scuttle, tin plates and cups, squat black coffeepot, strips of jerky and sack of flour—presently he completed his inventory, and spoke aloud in a murmur:

"A man wouldn't leave all this behind."

It could mean only one of two things. Either the horse-hunter had gone elsewhere with his herd seeking grass, which was unlikely, or Chacon had been here.

It suggested to Mossman that, if he were to search the ground outside, he might find a fresh grave.

It was more positive evidence than any he had yet seen, to prove the outlaw had been here. He went out into the chill wind to lead his horse into the little barn, unsaddle and feed it, and rub down its coat. Then he returned across the yard, bracing his body against the thrust of the wind, and took his saddlebags inside, where he built a fire in the stove and watched its red glow through the thick isinglass window; and made his spare supper.

When the fire went out he rolled up in a pair of blankets, slumping back in the leather-seated chair. He forced his eyes shut, and after a while drowsed. He heard muffled laughter in his dreams.

He was awakened abruptly by the sharp crack of a gunshot, not far away. Instinctively he rolled out of the chair, and snatched up his rifle. The door was still shut; no one was in the room with him. The stove was still warm. The shot must have come from outside—perhaps a signal.

He went to the door and opened it only a crack to peer out. Just then he heard another shot—it seemed to be a rifle, some distance away; and when he looked down the hill he saw the tiny figure of a horseman advancing at a trot.

Mossman stayed where he was, touching his gun. The oncoming rider stopped a hundred yards away, pointed his rifle in the air and fired a third shot, after which he put the rifle away in its boot and rode forward again, his hands lifted to the level of his chest. The rider was short and thin and round-shouldered. Mossman waited for him to come close enough for recognition. That was Billie Stiles, Burt Alvord's partner.

Mossman stepped outside, keeping his rifle ready. "Step down," he said.

Stiles dismounted and went ahead into the cabin. Mossman shut the door and moved across the room to stoke up the fire. Stiles was getting out of his coat. He said: "I didn't want to bust in on you at night, so I waited. Don't pay to startle a man."

"Good idea," Mossman muttered.

"We've got it set up for you."

Habit was too deeply ingrained; Mossman did not show his surprise. He only turned slowly, regarding Stiles with level blankness. "Where is he?"

"Camped with Burt—Burt Alvord, that is—on the side of San Jose Mountain."

"Up near Naco, that is."

"Sure enough," Stiles said. "Not more than five miles below the Border."

"All right," Mossman said. He took the battered coffee-pot outside and scooped up snow in it, and came inside to set it on the stove, spilling coffee into it. "Give me the details."

"We told him about the horse herd of Colonel Greene's. The horses are penned up just outside Naco, on the Arizona side of the line, just like you said they'd be. We told Chacon that this was your play and you'd ride along with them. Your name's Tom Nelson."

"All right," Mossman said, watching the stove. "Is he suspicious?"

"Chacon?"

"Yes."

"He's always suspicious. You got to be quicker than a bumblebee with that hombre."

"Go on," Mossman said.

"I said you'd join them not later than tonight."

"All right," Mossman said again. The coffee was steaming and he poured two cups. "Any more?"

"Just watch that son of a bitch. Watch him close. You never know when he's goin' to jump you—he might decide to jump all of us. He's got the guts. Which brings us to one other thing. How do we know we can trust you?"

Mossman sipped his coffee, watching Stiles over the rim of the cup. He kept his gaze grave and expressionless. "You can always pull out of this, Billie."

"Yeah," Stiles muttered. "Well, watch him close, hear?"

"That's unnecessary advice," Mossman said.

They rode out in a snow drizzle, well fed from the horse-hunter's larder. The day soon cleared, but it clouded up again toward noon, and light snow was drifting down again by two o'clock. They entered the chaparral flats east of the San Jose peaks shortly thereafter under a sky gray from horizon to horizon. Wind swept the plain, carrying flurries of snow and straws. Mossman kept his attention divided between the passing points of possible ambush and Billie Stiles; he trusted neither of them.

They were half out of a shallow canyon when a horse, whinnying through the evening dimness, made him halt and whip up his rifle. The sound had come to his ears on the wind; now he indicated to Stiles that they would get out of the open, and turned up the slope into the face of the wind, threading the brush to get cover, and settling down to motionlessness.

The horse signaled again; hoofbeats telegraphed along the ground and presently a pair of riders appeared on the floor of the canyon below. Billie Stiles said, "That's them."

"All right," Mossman said. "You first, my friend."

Stiles gave him a glance full of dry malice and seemed about to object; but then he put his horse downslope.

As soon as Stiles and Mossman came out of concealment, the riders below drew rein and waited with obvious suspicion. "It's all right," Billie Stiles called forward. "It's all right."

In answer, Burt Alvord lifted his hat, displaying the glistening baldness of his head. Mossman kept his hand on his rifle and a stern screen over his face; he followed Billie Stiles closely and watched all three of these men with infinite care, sensitive to all the little signs of possible trouble.

"This is Nelson," Stiles said, and drew up beside Alvord.

Mossman nodded. His gaze lay without expression on the face of Augustin Chacon, *El Pelado*. The trail of the outlaw had reached its end.

CHAPTER XVI

VICTORY'S PRICE

Chacon was lean and dark, almost black. His features were sharply cut and even. His shoulders were long, his chest was flat and wide, and his hands never strayed far from his cross-shell-belted guns. He said nothing; he did not blink. His eyes were only slitted suggestions in the dimness, but Mossman knew that Chacon was matching his own cool appraisal. It was the first time he had been face to face with Chacon.

Burt Alvord said: "The thoroughbreds are there. I had a look this afternoon."

"Then we'll ride now," Mossman said. "Those are some of the best horses in Arizona. Tonight's as good a time as any to run them. We'll cut the fence east of Naco to get them through. My judgment is that by morning we'll have them twenty miles into Mexico."

Chacon's thin hand lifted and his hat brim rose; he was still watching Mossman. He said smoothly, "No. Not tonight, *amigos.*"

Mossman stiffened. "Why?"

"*No podemos,*" Chacon muttered. "*Está obscura, la noche. Necesitamos mas lumbre.*"

"Hell," Mossman muttered. He thought, *What do you need more light for? You've stolen horses at night before.* His impatience was more than a part of the act he was putting on. He knew Chacon was stalling; he knew Chacon wanted more time to size him up before agreeing to pursue the plan; he knew Chacon was suspicious of him. But there seemed little choice. "All right," he said. "We wait for morning. But I don't like it. Daylight raid—that's dangerous business, gents."

"We will wait," Chacon said in Spanish. "We will make camp here."

Mossman had to acquiesce. It was his plan, if it proved possible, to get Chacon across the Border before throwing down on him. But he knew one other thing: whether or not Chacon backed out of the planned raid, he would be brought down within twenty-four hours, or he would bring Mossman down. The trail had been too long and too heartbreaking to allow it to take up again.

Mossman dismounted and hobbled his horse, making it plain by his attitude that he was dissatisfied. He took his rifle with him and crouched under the scanty protection of a mesquite tree, watching through half-lidded eyes the activity around the growing campfire. Chacon's glance was bright and malicious. Mossman could trust none of these three men; he knew the unsteady characters of men like Alvord and Stiles, and put no faith at all in them. It would be almost as great a victory for them to cut him down as it would be for him to capture Chacon.

He stepped to the fire to dish himself a tin plateful of *frijoles,* and stood looking down at the three outlaws hunkering around. Burt Alvord looked up at him and frowned in a warning way; Billie Stiles said: "Simmer down, Tom. Those horses will still be there come mornin'."

"I just don't aim to let them die of old age before I get them," Mossman said in a gruff tone. He cast a direct glance at Chacon, who returned his look blandly; and went back to his post under the tree. While he ate he kept his attention on his companions. He couldn't escape the feeling, unfounded as it was, that Chacon's level, constant look was one of half-concealed amusement; he couldn't escape the feeling that this man Chacon was laughing at him. He thought, *What's wrong? Get hold of yourself.* He was highly surprised by himself; deep in his mind he heard the muffled sound of a man chuckling.

Chacon stood up and scraped his tin dish clean with sand; he took his blankets and retreated a little way from the fire, and bedded down there, seemingly unconcerned. But Mossman's eyes noticed immediately that the man's hand lay only an inch or two from his cocked rifle.

With a display of indifference, Mossman rose and took his rifle up the hill to its summit, making plain his intent to keep watch. Below in the gully, Stiles and Alvord tended to the horses and then came back to stretch out in their blankets.

Stillness settled over the land. Mossman saw, on the

far side of the hill, the tops of crowded trees growing far below. He saw patches of glistening rock and snow, and the groined creases of canyons cutting back, and, farther out, the warm darkness of a timbered river meadow and the vague silver of flowing water. He wondered if the snow would begin falling again. The scent of conifers was a lie; it was so much kinder than the land that bore it. The vista all around was a beautiful uplifting of land, some verdant and some snow-blanketed, and that too was wrong; he felt it should have been ugly. He felt crouched hostility gathered in the hills and he heard harsh, rattling laughter, and moved mechanically, deliberately when he shifted positions to a rock from which he could see all three of the toughs below. The clouds had broken but they might tighten up again. The laughter echoed again and his mood turned harder; he viewed himself with some irony, which was a highly unusual thing. He sat showing his teeth; there were beasts growling in the land. He knew it was his thinking, and he was troubled by the disorder within himself, and by the impossibility of making sense out of the new questions that had risen to confront him. There was only one law that did not fail—survival; yet it seemed so senseless. He could catch, at times, the distant colors and sounds of other wonders; but none of them lasted, none of them outside himself had any meaning. A man believed in himself; he believed in not much more than surviving. There were always alternates; one alternate must always survive.

The entire answer, he felt, was death. Every man was born to die. He lived with a fear of it or a fight against it, or an acceptance of it. The first instinct was self-protection; then hunger, then pain; later came loneliness and fear, and then the curses of reason. But a man who could control his reason by his will, rather than by the force of outside wills, was able to survive.

A man who could kill without fear, he knew, had to be a man unafraid of dying. That was why it took a Burt Mossman to match an Augustin Chacon. He had to be a man equally unconcerned with the act of dying and with death itself.

He had often thought of death; he knew of it only as an absence, not a beginning and not an ending, but simply the existence of nothing. He had no questions about it and no uncertainties. Death was an unawareness; and a man unaware could not fear, or feel pain. Men feared death because they did not know what it held; Mossman did not fear it, because he knew what it did not hold.

Thunder crashing across a distant mountain startled him. He looked up and searched the camp, and settled back in a rigid position, unwilling to allow himself to become comfortable; he spent the night that way.

In the gray mist of dawn the camp came to life. Mossman stood and stretched his stiff muscles, and climbed down the hill. Billie Stiles and Chacon crouched near the fire. Burt Alvord came forward leading his saddled horse, and said, "I'm going down to the creek to get some water." When he walked past Mossman he said in a very low tone, "Billie's a back-stabber. Keep your eye on him." Then Alvord mounted his horse and trotted away. Mossman's head turned; he watched Alvord's huge shape disappear out of the gulch. He knew he would not see Alvord again; Alvord had played his part of the game and would get out now while it was safe to do so. Mossman nodded and continued into camp.

Stiles had a jackrabbit skewered on his rifle's ramrod, held up over the fire by two forked sticks. He pulled the ramrod away from the fire and ripped joints off the rabbit. Chacon took a leg and gnawed on it silently, watching Mossman steadily all the while. Chacon sat cross-legged with his rifle in his lap and it occurred to Mossman that Alvord, in leaving the camp, had probably made Chacon all the more suspicious. Chacon just now was most likely reconsidering his situation.

Billie Stiles squatted with his cup of coffee and said, "Them horses is waitin', boys."

"No," Chacon said, not lifting his voice. "We will forget it."

No one had moved; but Mossman knew at once that Chacon was waiting for the chance to kill him. Chacon had made it plain enough that he saw through the intended trap. The outlaw's black, narrow eyes now regarded Mossman with sharp heat. But behind it all, Mossman could see the hint of laughter.

Mossman took a red-tipped twig out of the fire to light his cigar. Over the wisp of smoke he looked searchingly at Chacon; he knew the time must be now. He thrust the twig back into the fire and during that instant, while he seemed off guard, he palmed his revolver and whirled on Chacon.

"Lift your hands," he said quietly.

Chacon did not move. His eyes flicked to Billie Stiles, who crouched without moving a muscle, and back to Mossman. Mossman stepped back a long pace so that he could command both men with his gun. In this split interval of time, he was in deadly danger; he had no way of knowing which way Stiles would turn.

He moved his gun barrel a fraction of an inch. "Up," he said again.

Chacon's arms rose slowly. Mossman reached into his pocket for a pair of steel handcuffs and tossed them through the air to Billie Stiles. "Put them on him."

Stiles moved carefully, walking around behind Chacon and drawing the man's upraised wrists together. Mossman heard the locks click into place.

The rifle still lay cocked in Chacon's lap. Mossman's breath was hung up in his chest; this was the end of it all, the accomplishment of the job he had been hired to do. Chacon's eyes stared at him bleakly. Mossman said to Stiles: "Pick up that rifle by the muzzle. Toss it away."

Stiles paused; Mossman's jaws tightened, rippling; and Stiles leaned forward to obey the command, lifting the rifle slowly from its position across Chacon's lap, and tossing it on the ground ten feet away.

"Now," Mossman said softly, "get rid of your own gun, Billie."

Stiles' mouth opened. "What the hell?"

"I'd be a fool to trust you, Billie."

"Why," Stiles said, "you're a God-damned son of a bitch."

"Maybe," Mossman said levelly. "Unbuckle your gun belt—drop it."

"Jesus," Stiles muttered, and loosened his belt, letting it fall. "You jailin' me too?"

"No. I made a deal—I'll stick by it. Cut out your horse and ride away from here. You can come back for your guns. I'll leave them here, without any ammunition."

Stiles stared at him with both anger and confusion; then he swung on his heel and walked away from the fire.

Mossman looked down at Chacon. When he met the out-law's eyes he felt again that Chacon was laughing at him. Chacon said quietly, "Well, Mossman."

Mossman made no answer of any kind. Chacon said, "I think I was a fool." But his lips spread back from his teeth in a tight grin, and he stretched his hands against the handcuffs. "Do you think you can get me as far as Arizona?"

"I think I can," Mossman said tonelessly. Chacon laughed. Mossman saw Billie Stiles riding away down the gully; and presently, when Stiles was out of sight, he prodded Chacon to his feet and herded him across the clearing to the horses. "I think I can."

Cackling laughter drummed against his ears. He let out all the air from his lungs and took a long breath; he raised his arms and touched the rifle trigger, with the muzzle aimed squarely at the center of Chacon's wide back bobbing in the saddle before him. But it could not be done like that. He took his finger away from the trigger and put the rifle in its boot. Chacon's head swiveled and he looked back, and said, "Why didn't you do it?"

"No," Mossman said. "You knew I wouldn't."

"As you wish," Chacon said, and turned his lean face forward again. His legs were lashed down tight against the horse's belly; his hands were cuffed together and a rope ran from the bridle of his horse to Mossman's saddlehorn. The clouds were retreating, dissolving overhead. Moss-man distinctly heard the outlaw's chuckle, quite soft.

Mossman gigged his horse alongside and said, "It's a long ride to Benson. You might as well relax."

"Yes," Chacon said, and grinned. "A very long ride, Captain."

Chacon's red eyes were fixed upon him. Mossman said, "You could have made a try at me back in camp."

"I could have," Chacon said. "It would have been a shame. And I wasn't sure who you were."

Mossman drifted behind him again and kept his wary attention on the wide, swaying back. Trees jogged past; they put their horses around a rock corner, broke out of the tangle of hills and entered the plain. It was a vast and lonely stretch of ground, all monotonous little sandhills sparsely rooted with bristling cactus and scrub mesquite and cholla. The soil was stony and the horses made some racket crossing the unprotected open. Around them, at varying distances, rose the violet raggedness of the high peaks. Laughter, thin and brittle, rode around insistently in Mossman's skull. He said, "That's the Border up ahead."

"I know," Chacon said in a tone of slight contempt; then his voice calmed. "Was it worth two years of it, Captain?"

"One day, or two years—nothing changes," Mossman said. "It was worth it. You're a part of my job, Chacon."

"And now you'll see me hang."

"No," Mossman said, and felt the wind, thin as a blade, cut through his clothes.

"You're scared to watch me hang, I think," Chacon said.

"No," Mossman said. "You know better."

"Sure," Chacon replied. He laughed loudly. "It has been a hell of a lot of fun, *mi amigo*."

Mossman spoke no more. Chacon turned suddenly; "Give me a gun," he said. "Let's have this out—the two of us—let's make it clean. I want it ended. It has dragged on too long."

Mossman shook his head. It was only the talk of a desperate man; he had to ignore it. Chacon's laughing subsided and went silent, and abruptly Mossman knew he had won. His uncertainties went away and he was left only with the conviction that he had been right, all the time he had been right; he would never doubt again. Chacon uttered a single terse word and fell into morose quiet. There was no more laughter. Mossman kept his face blank. Nothing had changed; he had a prisoner to deliver, and then his job was done, completed satisfactorily; his pride was satisfied.

They crossed the Border and rode straight through the night and into the morning, and finally topped a last hill. Below them, on the plain just below, sprawled the quiet buildings of Benson town, on the railroad. A train, up from Douglas, was just chugging into the depot. Mossman put his horse down the gentle slope, pulling the lead rope of his prisoner's mount. They rode into Benson, eliciting little curiosity from pedestrians abroad on the street. Mossman dismounted before the Southern Pacific depot and lifted a hand in greeting to a man on the cinder platform—Jim Parks, sheriff of Graham County.

"You're a welcome sight," Mossman said.

Parks's burly, gray-topped head rose and his eyes showed wonder. "Chacon."

"He's yours," Mossman said; he looked at his prisoner without emotion.

Parks moved down the steps to begin untying Chacon's feet. "It's been a long time coming to this pest."

Chacon spat on the ground and gave Mossman one last

glance full of hot anger; he shook off Sheriff Parks's hand
and walked steadily into the depot. Mossman waited until
presently Parks reappeared. "Locked up tight as he can
be," Parks said with some satisfaction. "It's been a long
hunt, Captain."

"Long enough," Mossman said, lighting a cigar.

"Where'd you get him?"

"Does it make a difference?"

"It might. If, say, you caught him in Mexico."

"Then just tell them I didn't say where I found him."

"He'll probably tell us," Parks said.

Mossman rammed his hands in his pockets and allowed
his cigar to jut upward at an angle from his teeth. "Will
you believe him?"

"I don't know."

"All right," Mossman said, and began to turn away.

Parks touched his shoulder. "Where to now, Captain?"

"A bath," Mossman said. "Some clean clothes, and then
a train ticket."

"Where to?"

"New York," Mossman said imperturbably. "I've got a
business meeting with Colonel Greene."

"Well, then," the sheriff said, "good luck, Cap." He
offered his hand. "Maybe we won't see you again."

"Maybe you won't," Mossman said evenly, and shook
Parks's hand.

"Funny," Parks said, looking upward. "Not a cloud in
sight. Not even in the south. I never saw a day this clear
and yet this cold. Damn near freezing."

Mossman turned away; he grasped the reins of the two
horses to lead them down the dusty street to a stable.

Twilight ran red over the hills and the street would soon become a black gully with flickering squares of lamplit windows and doors. He walked slowly, forming his future, discarding his gun; the time of the gun was past.

AFTERWORD

On November 21, 1902, Augustin Chacon was hanged on an Arizona gallows. At the time, Burt Mossman was in New York City with his friend Colonel Bill Greene of the great Cananea mine and ranch; Billie Stiles and Burt Alvord, the only other witnesses to the fact that Chacon had been kidnapped in Mexico, did not appear at Chacon's trial.

When he left Arizona, Mossman left it cleaner and safer for his having been there; but he did not leave as an unchanged man. Never again did he pin on a badge; never again did he take up the gun. He had done his job; he turned to new jobs. He lived on until 1956, rising through the wondrous cattle industry to become one of the few real tycoons of American stock raising; before he died, the modern American West had come into its own, and Burt Mossman had a part in it.

The amount of poetic license allowed an author of a historical or biographical novel has never been clearly established. I have taken liberties in the presentation of the character of Burt Mossman; I have created characters (like Santee and Ellen and a few of the minor characters) who did not exist at all. It must be emphasized strongly that this book is a novel, not a historical treatise; it should never under any circumstances be considered a source of factual material. Some of the scenes I have presented, like the last chapter, are very closely based on fact. Other scenes (for example, Chapter X) are only loosely suggested by historical events. From a factual point of view it is easy to find fault with my warping of dates or places, with my attributing certain fictional characteristics to real persons like E. S. Ives and Judge Starr Williams. Some of my historian friends can criticize this book because there is no mention of Mossman's friend Frank Wattron of Hashknife, or of other prominent men of the day.

To these men I say this: for absolute history, go to a history book. In anthologies of Western fact articles, in magazines, in the files of the Arizona Pioneers' Historical Society, in old newspaper archives—in a dozen sources one can easily find the facts as they happened, without embellishment and without interpretation. As a novelist I can lay claim to the novelist's right to search beyond bare facts, and the right to keep faith with facts only insofar as they form a part of the greater truth—the truth that was Arizona, the truth that was the conflict between genuine intelligent individualism and modern collectivism, the truth when the time of the gun was passing, the time of order arriving; the truth of how the land was tamed.

—b. g.